I0760962

A DISTRACTION TO DIE FOR

BONNIE ELIZABETH

My Big Fat Orange Cat Publishing

A Distraction to Die For
My Big Fat Orange Cat
Mystery 2020

My Big Fat Orange Cat Publishing
MyBigFatOrangeCat.com

ISBN: 978-1-953363-00-8 Trade Paperback
978-1-953363-07-7 Large Print

Chapter 1

The screech of metal against metal when the semi-truck overturned echoed around me. It'd been a near miss for a small white truck that raced off up the highway, narrowly missing being hit by the semi it had cut off. White truck driver forced a black truck into the deep ditch on the far side of the road, all without a backward glance.

Other cars further up the road from me slid off or were forced off into the shoulder. There looked to be one car under the semi. It didn't look good for that driver.

I'd been far enough back to avoid the accident. Fortunately, my charcoal gray Honda Fit had good brakes or I could have been one of the people sitting in the ditch. Instead, I pulled off to the side. I had to see if I could help. I might not have traditional medical training, but as an acupuncturist I was required to keep up with basic first aid.

The light drizzle dampened my clothing. No doubt the damp had contributed to the accident. The angle of the curve upon which the roads met was another issue, something that came up regularly in any Seales discussion about traffic. My father was considering a run for town council and he'd been looking up issues, so I was well aware of the problems at this particular intersection. Not to mention, my boyfriend, Byron Cabot, was a detective here in Seales, and he, too, knew the problems of this junction.

My acupuncture office was up a slight incline in a small strip mall that sat alongside the road where the accident took place. I was on my way home from work that evening. The angle of the sun hitting metal on the cars practically blinded me. Perhaps the truck driver hadn't even seen the semi, though it was hard to believe he had missed it.

I pulled out my phone to call 911, though I had no doubt that half a dozen other people were also calling. I saw Deena Reynolds come out of the pizza place and look out at the highway where the accident happened. She, too, pulled a phone from her apron and started dialing. A few other people followed behind her, probably getting a closer look at what had happened.

Seales, Kentucky, isn't a big town. In fact, it's downright tiny, making nearby Versailles in Woodford County look almost like a city. Frankfort appeared to be a huge city, particularly with the sprawl and growth that had been going on over the last thirty years or so. Sometimes I didn't even recognize my home.

I'm Ash Jericho. My mother's family has lived in Seales forever and even my father's family has lived in and around Kentucky for generations. My grandmother owned one of the local bourbon companies as well as a large plot of land that had once been used for horse farming. Like most areas just west of Lexington, our primary industry was farming, mostly horse farming, and we have our share of celebrity racehorses housed in barns nicer than many people's houses.

The county highway runs through the edge of Seales, heading towards Versailles in one direction and Frankfort in the other. The traffic light on the curve was for the road down to Lawrenceburg. There had always been accidents there and a few deaths, but this accident looked particularly nasty.

When the 911 operator answered, I reported the car accident on the highway and where it was.

"Are you injured?" she asked.

"No, I'm not. I was several cars behind the

semi. I'm going to go see if I can help. I have a medical background," I said. I clicked off before she could argue with me. No doubt the police and medics would be there shortly. In fact, I wasn't even to the first car when I heard sirens approaching.

The semi was on its side, the cab laying on the other side of the street blocking traffic from that direction. Dark marks on the pavement showed where it had slid across the far lane and off the shoulder and finally landed at the edge of small parking lot that held a generic dollar-type store. People in the store were coming out and talking with those in the thrift store. A bank sat a few car lengths away, and a woman outside had her hand to her chest, as if she'd worried she would have been struck.

On the opposite side of the street, near my office and the grocery store behind it, was the black truck that had been cut off. It had slammed into the grassy embankment below the little strip mall. A woman in a gray sweater was already pulling on the driver's door handle. A blue sedan and a white SUV were sitting at odd angles where'd they'd stopped—or tried to—to avoid the black truck. The sedan had another car tucked up under its smashed bumper and the SUV had an equally smashed bumper, though the car behind it had swung into the center of the road.

Naturally the accident had happened close to rush hour and there were plenty of people on the road coming and going between Seales and Frankfort or Seales and Lexington. No doubt a few were off to places further afield, perhaps even as far as Louisville.

I smelled gasoline and hot rubber. I hurried across the way to see if I could help the people in the cars. I wasn't the sort to leap up on top of the side of the semi's cab to try and get at the driver. I'd leave him for the professionals or for those who had a more athletic inclination. It's not that I'm weak or anything. I just didn't think my talents would be best used by climbing up the side of the truck.

"Are you okay?" I asked a woman in a sedan who was looking dazed. Her airbag had deployed and she was picking at the silvery white bag like she wasn't certain what it was. She was about my mom's age, wearing a seatbelt. Her hair was light brown, probably natural as it wasn't the sort of color you dyed your hair. Cut short, it was still messed up and there was already a slight swelling around her left cheek. I had a feeling she was going to bruise. She'd probably turned her head when she'd put on her brakes.

"I don't know," she seemed confused.

"Can you feel your fingers?" I asked, helping her move the airbag out of the way.

"I can," she said.

"And your feet?" I asked.

The confusion again. This could be a problem.

"Can you wiggle your toes?" I tried once more.

With that, she nodded. "I can!" Clearly she'd been worried that she wasn't sure how to tell if she could wiggle her feet. Either shock at what had happened or a slight concussion was keeping her from thinking clearly.

"Ambulances are on the way. You'll want to stay in the car, okay? Someone will help you further."

"I should get out though. In case someone else hits the car."

"No one else is going to hit the car," I said. "There's a car behind you and plenty of other people who have stopped."

The woman nodded at me, content to take my word for it. She rubbed the slightly swollen side of her face.

I hurried to the car behind her. Closer, I realized it was a gray Toyota Prius. The front end was smashed, suggesting the driver either hadn't had time to stop, hadn't been paying attention, or had been driving a bit too fast for the intersection.

A driver of it was a teenage girl and she was in

the seat, crying. She'd managed to move the airbag but she wasn't trying to get out.

I tried to pull on the door, but I couldn't get it to open. I felt the door move slightly and that was it. It was going to take someone with more strength than I had to open the door. The girl looked at me, still crying. She looked to her right and I saw her passenger was sagging forward. The airbag there had deployed but it looked as if the person—I couldn't tell from here whether it was a man or a woman—had lost consciousness. I ran around the back of the car to the other side to see if that door would open.

"Looks bad," said a man hurrying up from the line of cars back there. He was helping someone to the side of the road. I noticed that a few other cars were damaged, small dings and scrapes as if they'd mostly stopped, but not quite.

I pulled on the passenger door and this squealed open with just my strength. The passenger, a longhaired young man, I saw, started as if he'd fallen asleep and was just being woken.

"What…?" he trailed off, looking around, trying to make sense of what had happened.

"Stay still," I said. "There's been an accident."

The girl next to him continued to cry but now there was a level of relief in her tears. Looking at the car and where their legs were, I worried about their injuries.

Flashing red and blue lights caught my attention. Firetrucks, medics, and police arrived, converging around the accident, some from the north and some from the southwest, where Seales proper was.

An officer got out and started directing traffic while the medics went to work checking on people. The firemen started working on the semi's cab which lay on its side.

I stood up, stretching, letting the professionals get to work. I wasn't that useful, so I stepped off the road, walking back towards my car. I was always impressed with how tidy the roads looked.

The merchants in my office space all contributed to a fund which helped keep that area clean. A company came out to pick up trash and trim up the vegetation about once a month. A few years back when they'd put in the new sign that said "Welcome to Seales," the mayor had a push to clean up trash. Several of the church youth groups took turns cleaning the strip of highway between the sign to just past the junction. That meant the area was pristine.

That was why the crumpled white piece of paper caught my eye. It was also why I just naturally picked it up, not thinking. I'd been working with people, trying to ascertain what was wrong, so I had left myself open.

I'm psychic when I touch things. Not so much

humans, though I think it helps me read what's going on in their bodies and makes me a better acupuncturist, but with inanimate objects if I haven't shielded myself, I learn things. There were several times when I'd inadvertently moved something left behind by a patient and I'd learned far more than I felt I ought to know about someone.

Gram had taught me to shield myself and to not open myself to impressions. I was normally good at that, except around the clinic. It was something I had had to re-learn when I started practicing.

I was so flustered by the accident and what I had been seeing that I wasn't shielded. Besides, who thought a piece of paper would have so much emotion attached to it?

I felt anger, reaching up through my belly and into my head so hard that I thought my eyes would bulge out. I had no conscious thought of crushing the paper harder. I had an image of someone thinking a man should die, a young man with brown hair and eyes.

I saw him clearly. Blue jeans and a shirt, worn blue and white sneakers, possibly a hint of sock between the edge of the shoe and the sole towards the front of the right one. The jeans were nice enough, a bit faded. The shirt was light blue and black striped, button-down and loose. It was an odd look, not quite young man around town but not quite a working man.

His dark hair curled around his face and his oval-shaped eyes were hazel. I felt a hint of meanness in them, though whether that was actually true or part of the memory I couldn't have said. He wasn't smiling. The line of the lips again suggested cruelty.

I saw blood flying. Joy about it.

There was such a love of the blood and death that my fingers dropped the paper as I sat down on the ground.

"Are you okay?" a man asked.

I came back to myself, looking at an older man and a dog. Who walked a dog along this stretch of highway? After my initial shock, I realized that there were homes just beyond the highway and perhaps he was there to see what had happened. It wasn't like the accident was quiet.

The dog, a yellow lab, was well-behaved enough to sit by his owner and not go nosing at the paper. I picked it up again, making sure I was shielded. Even shielded, I felt hints of anger coming off the paper.

"I'm fine," I said. "Just needed to sit for a minute after that." I gestured out to the cars in the road. I heard the screech of metal as the firemen worked on the semi's cab. I heard the sound of people talking and yelling and still some crying. A few horns honked in the background, but most people were now aware of what was going on. Lots of folks were standing around watching.

"Good," the man said. "I heard it from my house. Called 911, of course, and then brought Jonesie up here. He's a good dog, comforting, in case anyone needed it. I'm not a doctor and I'm too old to be the guy who pulls people out—probably hurt myself trying—but Jonesie is good with snuggles and he's very polite. Figured it was the least I could do."

"Well, thank you," I said. "It certainly helped me. Jonesie is very polite."

I meant it too.

I crumpled the paper into my pocket, planning to look at it a bit later, once I could get out of the traffic jam that was piling up. I should probably just go back to work, but it was easier to sit there on the side of the road and watch.

Chapter 2

It was going to be late before I got home to Gram's—or should I say *my*— house. It was still hard to get used to coming into the big house and calling it mine though it had been for over a year, ever since Gram had died.

After the accident I got to watch a morgue truck take away the man in the small truck that had crossed into the ditch. I was already feeling melancholy, and then suddenly the choice of words about whose house had me missing Gram and remembering my own loss. Not that I ever really forgot she was gone, not for longer than a minute before I was reminded that I couldn't just ask her something when I needed to.

I had spent the afternoon watching things I'd rather not have seen. I'm an acupuncturist, which means I'm not totally squeamish when it comes to bodies and injuries. Gram might not have many horses, but when I was small my grandfather raised them and dabbled in breeding. I'd seen all kinds of things then.

Molly Jo, our new head groom, had suggested a ton of innovations. Right now we weren't utilizing all our pasture areas nor were we making use of the trails we had around the property. She was thinking about opening up certain spaces for trail riding, perhaps even a guided trail ride so we wouldn't have people wandering around the property.

Molly Jo was also keen on giving lessons. She had her own horse, which she had moved to our barn about a month after she started when one of our other boarders left. She said her mare was wonderful with kids and would be great for lessons, which she was willing to do.

She was already giving lessons to Win, one of the people who helped out around the house. I'd recently learned that Win was fascinated by horses but had been too afraid to ask about them. The fact that Molly Jo had jumped into offer lessons and showed such incredible patience with Win's embarrassment at her lack of knowledge endeared her to me—really to all of us at the house.

Jaci had been good, but she hadn't been willing to think outside the box. Well, maybe she had, but running drugs wasn't exactly what I meant about thinking outside the box. Because of her drug running, several people were dead. I am ashamed to say that I was thankful to know none of them well. One of the people murdered was a woman named Layla. She wasn't popular around town and was generally difficult. Still, she was a human being and deserved the respect of being mourned. That was true of the others who had been killed simply because they had all made poor decisions.

Everyone deserves a chance to atone, at least I thought they did.

While Jaci hadn't committed the murders, she had been involved with the drug running. That brought the crime closer to my home and my family than I liked. There was a part of me that was still angry with her. Her involvement had damaged our property, though fortunately not our reputation.

The worst for me was the loss of my beloved carriage house. It had burned nearly to the ground. I hadn't decided whether to rebuild it when Byron, the head detective I was dating, and Morgan, the property manager and houseman, decided it was going to be rebuilt. Morgan had put together some plans. Byron was contracting.

Byron is a detective, not a contractor, but apparently he's got a thing about building stuff. He's been out there on site most evenings working with whatever crew he could put together. The carriage house was going up nicely.

Byron had someone working on the roof the last few days. Apparently he didn't want to do that himself because he doesn't particularly like heights. I found that odd because he'd had no problems framing up the upper floor of the carriage house.

For months I'd been afraid to live there and now that I couldn't, it was the only place I wanted to live. Not just because of my relationship with Byron, which made me eager to have my own space, but because I was tired of having to make sure I was sufficiently covered to head to the bathroom.

This latest accident was going to slow the work on the carriage house, of course. It wasn't like Byron was going to be around to do whatever it was he was hoping to get done this week. Instead, there would be reports to write, statements to take, and perhaps even the unfortunate and sad job of notifying relatives of the death of a loved one.

I had seen Byron briefly at the scene. He had taken my statement about what I had and had not seen. Then he sent me on my way.

Other officers had been directing traffic. Tow trucks had arrived, weaving around the parked cars as the police started trying to get people through the jam. Many people were able to cut through the grocery store lot. As the day got later, I had no doubt that Deena's pizza place was going to be slammed.

Deena was the sort of manager who was smart enough to have called in extra workers once she saw what was going on. Her first call might have been to 911, but once she'd done her duty and reported, she'd probably looked up to see who she could call in. Naturally she'd have warned them to take the backroads.

Unfortunately, there had been enough accidents at that particular crossroads that Deena would be aware that clearing up the traffic jam would take a bit of time. People in a hurry would cut through the parking lot just behind her place to try and get home. She'd probably put up a sign advertising a special.

I was able to get my car turned around and take the back way to the house. It took longer than it should have, but once off the highway, my drive wasn't bad. My father was probably on his way home from Frankfort, so I gave him a quick call to let him know what was happening.

When I reached the house, I went upstairs to my room to look at the piece of paper I'd picked up. Everyone at the house knew about my gift, but I hated performing for people. It seemed like I was some sideshow act trying to make an impression, which was the opposite of what I wanted to do.

My room faces the front of the house, a nice room with a bay window that sat over the office downstairs. This was done in lavenders and blues, and my bright blue comforter, brought to go with the sunny yellows of the carriage house bedroom, actually managed to blend in, almost too much so.

I sat over towards a corner in a hard-backed chair I had brought for the little desk that sat there. I took out the scrap and spread the paper out. There was writing on it. I strained to read the words because the ink was so faded and smeared. I turned on my desk lamp so that I got direct light on it.

With the extra light I was able to make out the words, which had been scribbled in pencil by someone who hadn't cared about penmanship.

"Follow him. Make it look like an accident."

That was all. There was more, maybe a name, but I couldn't read it. I groaned. I was so going to have to call Byron about this. He knew about my gift, but he preferred to do his detecting the old-fashioned way, the way that he could take proof to the D.A. and get a conviction. A girlfriend randomly picking up a stray bit of trash and deciding to read it was going to be a tough sell.

I got up and lay down on my bed to think. My stomach felt tied in knots. I hated being involved in a murder. I had been involved twice before, once as a prime suspect and once as a slight suspect. I don't think anyone really believed I had killed Layla, but she had died outside my office. Now here I was with evidence that I didn't know how to turn in.

Times like that I really wished I could call on Gram's ghost.

I nearly jumped out of my skin when the phone rang just as Penelope Blue showed up on the bed, her little ghostly Siamese cat body sending a chill through me. Penelope Blue was one of my grandmother's Siamese cats from long ago. For some reason she hung around as a ghost and had a tendency to turn up when something important was about to happen.

I looked at the caller ID on my cell phone. Cheri. I smiled. At least Cheri knew enough about my talent to help me decide what to do. I picked up the phone hoping to tell her about what had happened.

Chapter 3

I stretched out on the bed as I pressed "answer" on my phone. I was on my back laying crossways, my legs dangling down, my toes just barely touching the rug on the floor. I missed the bright yellow and blue colors of the bedroom in the carriage house, but the lavender was nice. This was one of the rare rooms without green, which was Gram's favorite color.

I'd kept my blue comforter which had gone well with the yellow with touches of blue of the carriage house. I had laughed to myself often about needing things to match at Gram's, but I was glad it did. Back in Washington state, when I'd lived there doing acupuncture, I'd had mismatched everything. How things changed.

The bed creaked slightly as I leaned back on

it. Penelope Blue looked at me as if my stretching out had annoyed her. It probably had. Like all cats, Penelope Blue did not like to be moved, although whether or not I had actually moved her was in question. It's not like she had any mass. She did, however, step up and over me as if she were still alive before she glared at me while settling in to wash a paw, watching me.

Penelope Blue tends to only show up when there's something I need to pay attention to. Apparently Cheri's phone call was going to be important.

I pressed the answer button as the noises of the house around me settled into their usual familiar pattern. A click here or there from water flowing through the pipes. This late in the summer we didn't really need the air conditioning, and it wasn't yet cool enough for heat except sometimes first thing in the morning.

"Hey," I said, punching the answer button.

"I heard you were there this afternoon," Cheri said without preamble. "I cannot even believe you did not think to call me and make sure I knew you were safe and not one of all those folks who were taken to the hospital. Travis had the decency to call and let me know he was running late because they were still directing traffic even when he was off work!"

Travis was Cheri's latest boyfriend, someone I

was pretty certain she was going to stick with. He seemed to adore her. Cheri had asked me to touch a gift he'd given her, so I knew he was smitten.

I hoped his feelings stayed true because Cheri deserved a really nice guy. Of course, it had been months since I'd done the reading and he was still incredibly attentive to her—opening doors, carrying a drink, or pulling out her chair.

"Well, naturally I was there," I said. "I work right above where the accident happened. I'm not sure why you'd have thought otherwise. Being a healthcare provider, I did my good deed and went down and helped as much as I could."

"I heard you were in the car already." Cheri was doing her best imitation of a stern mother giving a warning.

"Well, okay, so I was on the road but just turning down the highway, and I had plenty of time to stop. I wasn't hurt, though a lot of folks were. I was going to call you later on. I didn't want to interrupt if Travis was there."

That was my latest excuse. While Byron and I were seeing each other frequently, Travis was an almost constant presence in Cheri's life. Maybe it was our different relationships, but I tried hard to focus on Byron when we were together, our various interests and businesses often keeping us apart. I didn't like to spend time chitchatting with someone else when he was there. Cheri seemed to have no such issues, though to be honest, because she spent most of her time with Travis, if she didn't talk to other people when he was around, she'd never do it.

I tended to let her call me in order not to disturb her. I really needed to get over that.

"If we don't want to be interrupted, we don't answer the phone," Cheri said, laughing. "But you're okay? And was it as horrible as I heard?"

"It was pretty bad," I said. "I didn't even see the principals, the guy in the semi and the guy in the truck."

"The man in the little truck was Duke Quint. He used to live here but moved to Lexington after college. He works for some engineering firm there. I guess he was on his way to see his dad when people up there say some other car nearly ran him into the semi and he had to turn quickly so he wouldn't go under the darned truck. Didn't help though, I guess. He died anyway."

I thought of the note and wondered if Duke was the guy mentioned in the note. Make it look like an accident.

I got up off the bed and went to the computer. No doubt there would be pictures of him. I wondered if he were a man with a slightly cruel smile.

"I didn't realize that was what had happened. I saw the white truck cross lanes and run another truck off the road. I didn't think he was going to go under the semi. The semi was busy avoiding the white truck too. I'm sure you heard it overturned. I think a different car hit the semi."

"It was a little Kia Rio and it got clipped a fair piece, spun around and ended up practically backing up under part of the trailer as the semi overturned. That was Kelly Ellis's car. I don't know if you remember him. He used to teach social studies in high school?"

"Really?" I said. I remembered Mr. Ellis. He was tall and quite blonde. He didn't look exactly like the image of the man in my sight but very close. He might have if he'd been younger. "I didn't even know he was still in town. I thought he'd left when he retired."

"He intended to," Cheri said. As a barista Cheri always had the latest gossip. She heard everything in the coffee shop and if she didn't hear it, she probably asked about it. Someone always came up with the information for her. She didn't talk too much about what she knew and if you asked her to keep a confidence, she was far better than you'd expect. I appreciated that about her.

"What do you mean?" I was looking up images. Duke had dark blonde hair and the smile wasn't quite right. He was much younger than Mr. Ellis, who was past retirement age.

I shuddered thinking about Ellis. He'd always

had that slight cruel look about him, and I hated it when I was the first one to class or the last one out. Fortunately, he never seemed to mind that the kids all came in in groups and didn't like being around him alone. He never held anyone back to speak with him, either. Like he knew.

"I guess he looked at places in Florida but that didn't work out, so he ended up back here. His house was paid for and he decided that it was just as good as he could get somewhere else. Plus, I hear his wife preferred Atlanta where their kids are. Their son is in computers, you know. Mr. Ellis thought Florida was just as close, but she wanted to be near her kids, or barring that, here. His wife is down there looking at houses, but those prices are just ridiculous and I've heard it's tough going, particularly if they want to be close to their kids."

Cheri prattled on about that for some time.

I was thinking about Kelly Ellis, still trying to decide if his face was the one in my vision. It wasn't impossible, but I couldn't be sure. It was, however, more of a possibility than Duke Quint.

I wanted the image to be Duke or someone close to Duke. After all, Duke's car was the one that went off the road when another vehicle had clipped the semi. Who could know that a car like Mr. Ellis's Kia would have ended up under a semi? For that matter, who could have known that Quint would be run off the road and die? He could have avoided the accident altogether, and then where would my angry person be?

Besides, if someone was trying to kill someone, they were just as likely to kill a lot of other people as their intended victim. It didn't seem logical to me, but thinking about it, I hadn't understood why Jaci hadn't gone to Gram with her desire to own her own home. It wasn't like Gram wasn't generous with her employees. Instead, Jaci had turned to a life of crime.

When Cheri took a break, as if she were going to change the subject, I jumped in.

"I had a weird thing happen while I was there," I said. I told her about the piece of paper and my flash. "It's a piece of garbage that someone threw out the window. My image didn't quite match Mr. Ellis as a young man, at least not from the pictures I'm seeing online, but the man really didn't look like Duke Quint."

"That's odd. I wonder if they were after the truck driver?" Cheri asked.

"What's his name?" I was ready at the computer about to type in. Fortunately, I had Cheri on speaker so it would be easy enough to do that. I'm rather old fashioned in that I still talk on the phone and don't just always text. I mean I do text most people and for quick things with Cheri, but when we're having a conversation, the phone is better. I'm not sure how Cheri would ever type out all the things she just has to tell me on a regular basis. It's almost nice that we don't FaceTime or anything like that, though we did Skype when I was in Portland.

"You know, I don't know, but I bet you could find out seeing Byron is on the police force," Cheri said.

"That's the thing. I want him to know about the note because maybe that accident wasn't an accident, but how do I tell him about the piece of garbage? I was just walking around and decided to pick up some garbage and the note looked interesting, so I read it? You can hardly see the writing. I had to work at seeing it. If I hadn't had the vision, I'd never have looked."

I felt like I sounded near tears, which was totally the wrong thing with Cheri. She'd probably throw on a pair of shoes and come right on over.

"I'm on my way over. We'll brainstorm there. Tell Win to make up a pitcher of that white wine sangria she makes with the peaches—or is it too late in the season for peaches?"

"We still have some. I think she was planning on canning them for us. Morgan found a deal at a you-pick kind of place. He took his grandkids out and they had a blast," I said. I'd heard about it later on and it sounded fun. When I was a kid, Morgan probably would have brought me, my brother, and my cousin, but as I got older, he treated me with more care and formality. Certainly he never felt that need with Gram, laughing with her and talking about things like her gift, but he'd lived in the house as her main assistant for decades.

Maybe next year I could get Cheri or Byron or perhaps both of them to go pick peaches with me. If Cheri brought Travis, we could make it a double date of sorts. Win could always find something to do with the fruit.

"I'm on my way," Cheri said.

I hung up the phone and went downstairs to ask Win to make up the Sangria. Penelope Blue glared at me as she leaped away, fading out as she did so. I hoped I'd listened and learned what she wanted me to pay attention to. So far I had been good about noting her presence and paying attention to the things she seemed to want me to. I had a feeling this would be a bad time to lose that focus and miss something.

Chapter 4

Cheri arrived long before full dark, and we went into the library. It's not a big room but it's cozy. It's next to Gram's office in the front of the house. Gram had decorated it with a couple of comfortable beige leather recliners near a window. A small rounded brown table sat between them, holding a lamp and leaving room for drinks or snacks. Bookshelves ran along the back wall, complete with a library ladder. Like most of the rest of the house, Gram had had the wood stained a very light stain, and the shelves and ladder were a creamy caramel color.

A small electric fireplace huddled against the wall with the door so you could make the room even cozier. It wasn't a very used room, but I had taken to it lately. It felt private. I knew if I wanted to use the great room and needed privacy, Daisy would have seen to it that I had it, but she enjoyed watching television in there or reading a book.

Gram's study was a business room, with only a couple of chairs and the desk. The function of the library was a quiet place to sit and read, or just to sit and be alone if the rest of the house was too noisy. Gram rarely used it when I was around. Usually she was out in the great room, but Morgan had told me that in the last year or so she had taken to often spending an hour or so in the library, reading or just petting her living Siamese cats, Hellspark and Babs.

Hellspark, the more outgoing of the two cats, poked his head into the library and joined us as soon as I turned on the electric fire. It made a small crackle sound as if it was the real thing. Babs was probably out with Daisy. When Babs got comfortable, she rarely wanted to move. Hellspark was far nosier and more active, hence his name.

"So tell me," Cheri said, once we were comfortably ensconced. The chairs faced the room but at an angle, so during the daytime you could easily turn your head and look out. At night there were cream-colored blinds that closed off the room from the outside. The rug in this room was a pale peach with cream geometric patterns. It was very tasteful and very modern, much more so than Gram normally did.

I glanced at the large painting of two Siamese cats above the fireplace. They were kittens playing together, one a dark chocolate point and the other a lilac point, their pinkish pads picking up the pale colors of the room and the reds from the fireplace. They weren't Gram's cats, just a painting she'd seen and fell in love with because of the subject matter.

"It might not be high art, but art should be things one loves, not something critically acclaimed," Gram said. "I supposed the critics are all just a bunch of people who have an eye for what is finely done so that others can follow their lead. Sometimes you just have to decide you want the cats."

Whenever I agonized over what to put on my walls in my acupuncture clinic, I always remembered Gram saying that. It was so very much her, and it gave me confidence in my own taste. After all, not everyone had to share it. It just had to reflect me.

The sangria smelled of peaches and oranges and the slight dry scent of the wine. Win was good at making this particular sangria, and it was one of Gram's favorites. Gram liked the red as well, but Win usually made that later in the year when peaches weren't around, at least not fresh.

"I just found that piece of paper." I had laid

the paper on the table, as far from the glasses of sangria as I could.

Cheri picked it up and read it. "It's definitely says to make it look like an accident. But you're right, it doesn't make sense that you'd unfold this and read it. It's all wrinkled and crumpled and the writing is so faint."

I nodded. "So you see why I'm hesitant to tell Byron."

"You told him about your talent. Tell him and then let him worry about the piece of paper. Maybe he could say he was looking around and found it or something. Even if he says you found it, which you did, if you were at the scene, unfolding the paper might make sense because people do all sorts of weird things when they're in shock, you know." Cheri made it sound so simple. Except it wasn't.

Cheri had known my grandmother, knew she was psychic and knew that people went to her for advice. Cheri confessed that her mother thought it was a bit odd, but no one had really cared.

The fact that I could do it hadn't really come as a surprise. Cheri had sort of known. We'd played together, and now and then I'd get a read on something and share things. After I got older and my mother learned about my talent, she had put a stop to me sharing my insights. She worried I'd be ostracized. As mothers do, she'd told me I'd lose all my friends, which scared me, so I'd hidden away what I could.

I had always thought Cheri had forgotten about my early lapses in hiding my ability, but in reality her mother had said that all kids made up stories, which was what I was doing. Cheri was told she shouldn't take anything I learned when touching something too seriously. Both of us had had a long talk about how both our mothers had played a role in the secret I had kept all those years.

At any rate, Cheri now just took it as a part of who I was, as if I'd learned to read items with my fingers while studying acupuncture.

If anything, she pushed me to use my talent, which wasn't always a good thing. We'd come close to being killed because she'd wanted me to find something of Jaci's in order to find out more about what was going on last spring. Fortunately, Byron had had police watching Jaci and they'd come to our rescue.

"Byron isn't exactly as accepting of my talent as you are," I said. "If I show him the paper, he might write it off as a joke. No amount of telling him I got a read will make him change his mind. I mean, if this were a personal thing, he'd be fine. It's not like he really disparages it, but he's not the sort to bring it into his professional life. He thinks I'm crazy for doing it in my office. He keeps talking about liability, or he did, until he had a treatment and realized that he'd never know if I was using my talent or not. I guess he thought I'd be more like a medical intuitive than just following where I felt I needed to place the needles."

Byron had been a surprisingly good acupuncture patient. Often the tougher the man, the worse he is about needles, but Byron was stoic. He'd also really liked the way he felt after. He hadn't exactly come running back for another treatment, but given our new relationship, it was probably all for the best. We were close, but not so close that discussing bowel movements was just another conversation.

"Would he investigate on his own and not tell anyone why?" Cheri asked.

I shrugged. "He might, but I doubt it. He'd have to explain why, so unless there's something else odd about the accident, then he's not likely to do it."

Cheri made a face. "He's an idiot. Dump him."

I made a face and waved a hand at her. She wasn't serious. Cheri just said things like that when she was frustrated.

"We know that someone was supposed to die. Two people are dead and neither of them looked like the guy in your vision, so maybe you saw a vision of the person who was planning their deaths, like when he wrote the note or something like that? I mean, it says make it look like an accident as if someone were being instructed, did that make sense?"

I nodded at her. Cheri was right. The face I saw could have been the person giving the instructions. The person who had tossed the paper could have been the angry person, but maybe I had picked up the face of the original writer of the note, not the target of their fake accident. If I was seeing the instigator, then it would make sense that neither of the people who had died in the accident looked quite like the man in my vision.

"It seems like Duke Quint was probably the target," I said. "I mean the way Mr. Ellis died was sort of just an unlucky moment. No one could have predicted how the semi would overturn short of some crazy wild movie."

"You're right. So it's likely Duke, assuming either of them was the target, but he's all we have, so we'll focus on him," Cheri said. "We can find out what we can about him and see if there's a reason someone would want him dead, though I can't say what it is because he's been in the area forever, but not much it town, really. His dad is here and Duke visits, but not that regularly, if you know what I mean, so whoever wanted him dead had to know him well enough to know his schedule."

"So, we'll look at who connects with him on social media and things." I took a sip of sangria. Wine made everything seem easier.

"You'll look at social media and get names. I'll talk to people at the coffee shop because you know even tomorrow this will be big news. It was a huge accident and everyone knows someone who was effected by it, so they'll all want to tell me what they know. If anyone knows the Quints, they'll be really excited to share what they know by being close to the family, although I have to be careful because there'll be grief too, and I don't want to seem like a monster. Still, you'd think it would be for a good cause because if someone did want Duke dead, you'd think they'd all want to know, right?"

Cheri made me smile a bit. She always runs on talking like she's a writer being paid by the word, but she usually makes sense. I have to admit, though, that sometimes it's a bit tiring.

"It sounds like a good plan." I made no move to get up, just sipping at my sangria which went down easily. I don't really get drunk easily, but wine makes me lazy and indolent very quickly. It's one reason I had Win make up enough for two glasses and no more. I didn't want to be too indolent.

Cheri and I talked some more while I got her to eat some cheese and crackers. I didn't want to take any chances that she was going to have an accident when she drove home. I even had Win bring us some herbal tea as our evening wound down. Normally I'd have just let Cheri go because she knows her limits, but having just seen how bad a car accident could be had me on edge. Plus Byron was always telling me to watch my driving.

"I'm a detective and it looks bad if I'm with someone who breaks the law. It's why the department was sketchy when you were implicated in Layla's death," he had told me. I wanted to honor that. I'd hate it if he didn't take my work seriously, so I took his that way, even if it meant pushing herbal tea on Cheri when she was ready to go. It was a particularly selfless move on both Cheri's and my parts because Cheri doesn't much drink herbal tea.

As I said goodbye, I turned to go inside and start my computer search. I didn't want to look too long because I had patients the next day. I wanted to get to bed early so I had good night's sleep, not that that happened, of course.

Chapter 5

Duke wasn't a big social media user, which meant I spent far more time than I should have on my computer. As a result, I ended up tired and grumpy in the morning. I couldn't find my favorite shirt, which I thought would have made the day nicer. It's a soft blue and fits me perfectly. It moves with me, so I can easily lean and move when reaching across patients or helping them onto the table.

Finally, I found it in the bag of laundry. I needed to put the bag out for Morgan and Win to do. I kept intending to do my own laundry, but for some reason I always put it off. I had started out with a routine, but the longer I lived in the big house, the worse I got about doing my own chores, increasingly relying on someone else to take care of me.

I needed to stop that. While I was still nervous about living alone, even just across the driveway in the carriage house, I would be glad to get back there. I needed to have my own life and have some semblance of self-reliance. I already made sure that Morgan had had the designer put in a small laundry room for me. Byron had shown me where it would be as he framed it out. Plumbing would go in soon. The room wasn't large and was in the back of the carriage house. It would even have a small window.

I'd decided to have the front-load washer and paired dryer stack on top of each other so I could have a bit more floor space. I was used to living with cats. Floor space in a laundry room is prefect for a litter box. Chances were I wouldn't be moving with Babs or Hellspark. They weren't young cats any longer and were used to the large footprint of Gram's house. Besides, I was fairly certain Babs had bonded with Daisy and wouldn't appreciate being separated from her. There was also no way I could separate her from Hellspark, either. Which meant I'd soon be in the market for my own cat. While I love Gram's Siamese, I don't really have a preference for breed.

Once I had my own laundry space, I'd even wash my own clinic laundry instead of sending it out. Morgan thought I was silly for doing so when he and Win could have done it, but I didn't want to make them work for my business as well as for me in the house. I needed to keep business and personal separate.

I left the favorite shirt in the bag and grabbed one of my other casual but not too casual shirts. This one was a black sweater type thing with three-quarter length sleeves. I put that on over khakis and slipped on shoes. I was ready for the day.

It was only Wednesday, so I had a few days before I'd have the weekend to go sleuthing. I mentally figured out my patient load. It had increased in the last few months. Today I had five patients scheduled, which had become usual for me. I'd like to get up to ten patients a day so that I could drop back to three and a half days of seeing patients. The other half day I'd do paperwork.

I ate yogurt and nuts for breakfast. Win was always willing to make me something heartier, but I wasn't a big eater in the morning. I just put some of the chopped up fresh peaches and a handful of walnuts into the plain yogurt that Morgan picked up for me at the store.

The weather was cooling off, so I'd probably switch to eating oatmeal soon. Or once I was in the carriage house, I could make myself some eggs. I preferred the protein in the morning to the carbs. I didn't get tired halfway to noon.

Driving to work, I considered what I did and did not know about Duke Quint and why someone might want to murder him. I had looked through the pictures on his social media, all eleven of them. Fortunately, he wasn't one to keep everything private. He just didn't seem to care much about his account. What was a little odd was that no one else tagged him in photos with them, either.

I'd learned that his mother had died a few years ago. Duke had a sister, but I couldn't find much information on her. She had accounts at all the sites I checked, but they hadn't been active in a couple of years. When she had been, she'd often tagged Duke in her posts. He said nothing about what had happened. That also struck me as a bit odd, but then again, he clearly wasn't a social media user.

Duke worked for an engineering firm. His title was merely Engineer, which told me nothing about what he did. When I looked up the company he worked for, I learned they made small machine parts that were primarily used in airplanes. They contracted with the giant airline manufacturers and the government. I wondered if that meant there were other uses for those small parts that they weren't mentioning.

I didn't get the sense that Duke had many hobbies, at least not that he bragged about. There were two photos of him on a mountain holding a snowboard, smiling under a helmet, goggles raised up, the mountain in the background. The height and angle of the run he was on suggested an east coast ski area rather than west coast. Naturally, it wasn't tagged.

I paused in my memory to wait at the stop sign where I turned onto the highway to go into work. The traffic was running evenly on the highway. Clearly no one was slowing down to gape at the place of the accident. It's a busy enough intersection that I had to be alert for an opening and grab it. Fortunately, this morning I didn't have to wait too long.

There were days when I turned right instead of left and then made a U-turn at the next intersection about half a mile up the road. When I was in high school heading off someplace, I had never done that. I wasn't sure if it was that there was more traffic or living on the west coast had made me more impatient.

My stomach growled, reminding me that I hadn't quite eaten enough before leaving. I should have had one of the muffins Win had made the night before. I had one packed for a snack, but I was probably going to dig in as soon as I made sure all my treatment rooms were set up and ready to go.

Once on the highway, it didn't take me long to get to the office. I love the way my place smells. I sell herbs, mostly granules, but they still give off a certain smell that reminds me of my clinic and my home. I'd used moxa the other day, so the sweet smoky smell covered everything. It wasn't that bad, but patients would notice. I tried not to do too much of it even though I'd made sure my office was well ventilated and the scent wouldn't waft over to Deena's, perhaps putting people off their pizza. It can get pretty strong, the sort of smell that can lodge in the back of your throat.

When I'd mentioned it to her, Deena had stuck her nose in my office and taken a big whiff.

"Smells like you've been smoking something illegal." She'd laughed and added that if I was, I should send the patients over to her so they could get their snacks.

Joke though Deena might, moxa wasn't likely to make folks hungry no matter what it reminded her of. If anything, it was likely to make people less hungry.

I left the door open to air out the space. Soon enough the weather wouldn't allow me such luxuries.

I walked back down the long hall to check that I'd cleaned each of my treatment rooms. Of course I had, but I like to make sure. I also straightened things that I felt needed to be a bit tidier. I put my muffin in the break room at the back.

Back up front, I looked at the appointment book. Pam would be in at noon and was working until seven. She was the massage therapist who rented a room part time. For now, she had very flexible hours as the office was bigger than I needed. I figured as I got busier, we'd have to adjust so that her time in the office was more scheduled, so I'd know if I could use that third room for patients if I went over time.

She knew that was a change that was coming, so I wasn't worried she'd leave. I'd been so lucky to find her. If she'd threatened to leave, I think I'd have rethought how to work things so that she could keep her flexible hours. Patients loved her and she was very reliable.

I had just a few more minutes before my first patient. I drew in a few deep breaths to get ready for the day. I moved my arms in some tai chi motions to loosen up.

Just as I was thinking I was calm enough, Byron walked through the door. Byron is not my patient, except for that one experimental treatment. Byron does not normally visit me at work. In fact, the only time he ever "visited" was the time I found a body outside the office.

"What's up?" I asked, my heart fluttering. It could have been the way his very dark hair waved across his forehead and the slight crease when he pulled his lips back in a half smile. It may also have been worry that something had happened, and I was once again in the crosshairs.

"I'm going around getting witness reports on the accident and wanted to know what you observed," Byron said. He had a notepad computer that he was waiting to make notes on. I'd given a short statement the night before, but he had warned me I'd have to do something a little more formal in the next few days. Apparently he thought now was a good time.

"I was down in traffic, so I saw the small truck cross the lanes of traffic, veering away from the semi. I don't know exactly what happened. I pulled over to see what I could do until the first responders came. Then I stayed out of the way," I said.

Bryon nodded. "Did you notice what made the truck swerve?"

I had heard stories by then. I had read them. Everyone had, but I couldn't remember seeing anything when it had happened. "I don't think so. I mean I've heard stories, but I don't think I actually saw anything. I was too far back, far enough to stop easily and not slam on my brakes."

"I appreciate your honesty," Byron said. "Lots of folks would have tried filling in the blanks."

I shrugged.

I nodded at Mrs. Platt as she walked through the open door. She comes in for monthly sessions now. She had arthritis quite bad in her hands and wrists, but we'd been working together for some time. We'd found that if she came in about once a month, she stayed at a level she was comfortable with. She wasn't completely off her pain medications, but she'd been able to seriously cut back on the amount. I was eager to see how she did through the changing winter weather. I had already warned her that it was possible she'd need to come in more often for a short time when the weather changed.

"I don't suppose you had any psychic feelings?" Byron asked softly. That was an odd question for him.

"You don't think this was an accident?" I asked.

Byron reddened a little. He glanced over at Mrs. Platt and then shook his head almost imperceptibly.

"Morning," I said to Mrs. Platt. "Let's go on back to the room." I opened the door to the hallway that ran between my treatment rooms and gestured for her to come on back.

"I can see you're busy with that police officer.

He's a nice young man, don't you think?" Mrs. Platt said. She'd lived in Seales long enough to have her own hotline to any gossip circle in town. She had to know that Byron and I were dating.

I just smiled. Once I had gotten her to a room, I told her to get comfortable and I'd be right back. She's been a patient long enough to know the routine.

Mrs. Platt gave me a too large smile and watched me with birdlike eyes, too observant for her own good.

No wonder there were no secrets in Seales.

Once in the front office again, I folded my arms. "I picked up a piece of paper out there and got a sense that it wasn't an accident," I said. That seemed easiest.

"Why didn't you tell me?" Byron asked.

"Because, as I believe you've said, police work isn't about psychic feelings but about actual hard evidence."

Byron sighed. "Is that all, just a feeling?"

"And the fact that the paper said something about make it look like an accident," I said. "I have it at home. I was trying to figure out how to give it to you without sounding crazy."

"There's always a certain level of crazy about you," Byron said. "I think I need to see this paper."

"It's back home. In my room. I'll give Morgan a call and he can let you go up there."

It wasn't like Byron really needed permission. He hadn't been in my room. As I said, I felt like I was living in a group home and bringing a guy over for an overnight felt wrong.

"Thanks," Byron said, turning to leave. Not even a kiss. So much for closeness and for accepting my psychic abilities.

Chapter 6

I hated the way butterflies were fluttering around my belly and chest after Byron left. I didn't like the way he'd left things. He'd come in and asked for my general feelings, which included psychic impressions. At the same time he'd acted as if he didn't want to hear them. To top it off, he was annoyed that I hadn't immediately called him when I'd found the paper.

Maybe he'd realize why once he saw the paper. It wasn't as if it was a nice clean sheet of paper that anyone would have unrolled and looked at. It was a piece of garbage that I'd never have looked at a second time if I hadn't had the impression I had. If it hadn't been as strong as it was, I'm not sure I'd have looked at the paper.

I walked slowly down the hall, trying to calm

myself again. Mrs. Platt deserved the best from me. I breathed in the smell of the office, the smell of herbs in their containers, the faintest traces of moxa that would probably be there in a decade, and the clean smell of the fragrance-free laundry detergent I used. I tried not to use scents in the office at all, but there were natural smells that always took over a place.

I closed my eyes in the hallway outside the door to the room Mrs. Platt was in. I stood there, facing the white wooden interior door, and breathed for three breaths, concentrating on nothing else. When I opened them, I stepped inside onto the soft brown and green bamboo print rug. Mrs. Platt was lying on her back on the massage table where I would work on her. Background music came from a player in the corner, and stringed instruments offered soothing sounds and a bit of white noise.

"And how are you today?" I asked quietly.

Mrs. Platt smiled. "Well, I am starting to feel the cold. I was doing well until I went out to pull up a few straggling weeds. Suddenly my hands felt as if they were all knotted up. If I didn't have an appointment today, I'd have called in for one."

"When did it start?" I asked.

"Tuesday, actually," she said. "I used a heating pad because you said the cold might make it worse. It helped, but my fingers are still stiffer than usual. I took a few extra medications to get me through. Nothing this morning, though, so you could see where I am."

I nodded and rested my fingers lightly on her wrist to take her pulses. Her skin was cool to the touch and it was loose, without the elasticity in a younger person. Still, her eyes were bright and she was reasonably active, even if she couldn't always do her gardening as she wanted.

The pulses there were strong enough, though a little weak in her digestion location. That's common enough. I went to the other side to feel the pulses on the left, noting where there were imbalances. I looked at her tongue and wrote down what I had found.

I turned my back to her to wash my hands in the sink at the back of the room and to get needles.

"That accident yesterday was horrible. Poor Duke," Mrs. Platt said.

I tried to keep the smile off my face. This was just the kind of thing I needed.

"Did you know him?" I asked.

"I knew both of them. Kelly Ellis was a good man, or decent enough. Taught at school, though you probably knew that. I bet you're of an age to have had him."

I nodded.

"It's sad about him, but at least he had a life.

Duke wasn't very old, you know. He was an engineer. I doubt anyone expected him to make much of himself, so he surprised us all. As a boy, he was always a bit lazy. Going off to college changed that, it seems. Got some student loans and worked hard. Took him seven years, but he graduated. Community college in three years and then he transferred and took classes mostly part time while he worked. Lived at home a lot of that."

Mrs. Platt sounded very proud.

"That's a lot of work," I said.

"His father helped a lot. They were close. I can't imagine what he's going through."

"It must be horrible to lose a child," I commiserated.

"I had heard that he might be moving closer to home to help out his father. He's needed some care, I guess. Probably a hard decision because Duke loved living in Lexington. Much more his kind of place, though I'm surprised he didn't run off to Seattle or something where it's a real city, not like Lexington."

I wondered if there was some sort of censorship or admiration in her comment, considering I'd run off to Portland to go to school. I had only returned because of Gram's death.

As if reading my mind, Mrs. Platt tapped my hand just before I got the needles set to insert them.

"Not at all like you. Beverly always knew you'd come back. It was more that you needed to go out there to get the education you needed."

Mrs. Platt was quiet for a moment. "I worry about what will happen to Bud Quint now. His daughter isn't around."

"Was there a Mrs. Quint?" I asked, just interested, of course. I knew that Duke's mother had died, but wasn't sure if she'd been married to him or someone else. I found a point on Mrs. Platt's lower ankle. Her arthritis might be in her fingers, but points not local to her fingers were very helpful in keeping her issues at bay.

"Not for a few years. Breast cancer. So young, too, barely even fifty if I remember correctly."

Mrs. Platt was almost as good as Cheri when it came to ferreting out information. I was impressed.

"That's sad. Where's the daughter?"

"No one really knows. I heard she ran off to New York to try and make something of herself, but then never heard anything again. There were rumors of drugs and what not, but it's hard to say when she's so far away. Could just be that she didn't like her dad much. While he and Duke were close, it really wasn't until Duke was mostly through college that they got closer. Bud might have been a bit on the authoritarian side."

I smiled and continued inserting needles.

"I just can't believe it. It never gets easier when you know a young person who has died."

"Did you know Duke personally?" I wondered if perhaps I could get some information out of Mrs. Platt about Duke's personality.

"Just slightly. I know Bud a bit better though we aren't what you'd call close friends. He's just always been around the corner from us, you know. A neighbor and nice enough. Once in a while, if we got a fair amount of snow, he'd have Duke come by and shovel if my daughter's husband didn't get over to do it for us."

"That was thoughtful of him," I said. Particularly if he lived around the corner. Either that or Duke looked for excuses to get out of his father's house. I didn't know him well enough to know which was which, so I didn't comment.

"I thought so," Mrs. Platt said. Her voice sounded sleepy, and I finished the needling in silence, letting her drift away into what I and many classmates called "aculand," that nice, relaxed, near-sleep state of healing.

I made sure the music wasn't too loud and that the room was warm enough before I left. I'd go to the front office and make notes on what she told me, both about her health and my treatment and also about what she'd said about Duke and his family. It didn't mean a lot right now, but perhaps

Cheri would learn something that would help put that information into perspective.

It seemed like Bud wasn't always a nice man, but Duke was a dutiful son. Or maybe Bud hadn't raised nice children and he was the wronged person. Of course, how did that fit with Duke going to shovel Mrs. Platt's driveway?

More information was definitely needed. It was certainly possible that Kelly Ellis was the intended target. It could also be that if someone was targeted, they hadn't even been harmed, and Mr. Ellis and Duke Quint were what they called collateral damage.

Still, I wanted to know what the note meant by making it look like an accident. The writer or the receiver of that note was the person I wanted to find. The best place to start was with the men who were dead. Duke was the most likely target. The next most likely target was the driver of the semi that had been cut off. He wasn't a local man though, so it didn't feel likely.

Even if he had been, there had to be easier ways to try and kill someone than to try and overturn their rig. Those things were huge. And they offered a certain amount of protection, too. It wasn't like a small car running into them could guarantee the driver of the large truck would die.

No, Duke was the most likely person. So far he sounded like a good enough son with a father he was close to. Neither Cheri nor Mrs. Platt had told me about anyone Duke had problems with. It didn't mean those people didn't exist, just that I hadn't heard about them. I wondered who might know of someone who hated Duke.

I input Mrs. Platt's information into my computer while I waited for her treatment to finish. She still had a few more minutes. I moved over to my phone and started looking around on social media. Now that more people knew about Duke's death, I wondered if more people would be making comments on his profile.

I searched his name again. As expected, there were plenty of RIP type comments.

One stuck out for me. *Can't say I'm sorry you're gone but nasty way to go*. The person who said it was a man named Craig Roland.

That led me to search through Craig's account. He didn't have his account locked down as much as Duke. I easily learned that Craig liked beer, football, and baseball. He was not a fan of men kneeling for the anthem, nor was he a fan of people who wanted universal background gun checks. This concern seemed to take up an inordinate amount of space on his timeline, considering that there was no such legislation proposed. He was in a relationship with a tiny, mousy-looking woman named Stephanie Leads.

There was nothing specific about Duke on

Craig's timeline, so I moved to Stephanie's page. Unfortunately, she was another one of those who locked the general public out of her personal life. I only saw a few news articles that she liked, which gave me her political opinions. She did not seem to disagree much from Craig, though she didn't have quite the same number of articles, at least not for public consumption.

Stephanie had not hidden her friends list, which was fortunate. I was going to start searching those when I realized that I needed to go pull needles from Mrs. Platt. I set my phone down and got back work. It was going to take me some time to get back to searching her friends list for anyone else connected to Duke.

Chapter 7

Later that day, after lunch, I had another regular patient, Ryan Dushane. Ryan worked at the grocery store that anchored the shopping center behind my building. He always came around lunchtime. This time his appointment was just a bit after my lunch at 1:30.

Ryan worked different shifts, so he scheduled his appointments with slight irregularity. I'd been seeing him for back pain, but that had gotten better. Just last week he'd called about a shoulder injury. I'd set him up with several treatments to help that heal. This was his third one.

Ryan was in his thirties with short, dark-blonde hair and green eyes. He wasn't handsome in the traditional sense. He was a little too short, a little too plain, and a little too soft, though his work included lifting and bending and running around the store. He had a nice smile and his eyes always seemed interested in what people were saying. When he talked and listened, he became attractive, and I suspected he had a fair number of admirers. His paperwork did not indicate a Mrs. Dushane.

He was seated on the same table Mrs. Platt had been on. It was a lift table that I loved, and I had plain, cream-colored flannel sheets on it. Mrs. Platt had had green to go with the rug. I was going through my regular follow-up interview with Ryan, discussing his case as he sat there fully dressed. No one had been in the front of the office to keep me from talking to him right away.

Music still played softly in the background. It had changed to a synthesized nature music that was soothing. This particular piece always made me a little sleepy, and I hated that it was just starting as I was starting a treatment.

"I was able to do my usual work," Ryan said quietly, proud. "So it's really helping fast this time."

Ryan's back pain had been exacerbated by all the lifting he had to do for his job. He had to take a lot of care to get that to improve. The shoulder was easier because it was more acute and because he was already learning what he had to do to keep it from being re-injured. Or maybe he had just learned the consequences of re-injuring himself over and over again.

"But you shouldn't have been doing the full amount," I said. "While you'll heal faster coming here, you can't expect miracles."

Ryan gave me that nice smile and shook his head. "I'm not doing full lifting. It was just light stuff, not my usual. And it feels so much better. It's really great."

"I'm glad to hear." We went over his range of motion and pain scale. I also asked what else was going on.

"Going to a funeral later this week. You knew about that guy in the wreck, Duke Quint?"

I nodded.

"He was a friend of mine," Ryan said. His normally light eyes became shadowed even as he said it.

"I'm sorry for your loss," I said. "When did you hear?"

"I was at the store when it happened. I didn't even know until after I got home. That's weird for me, too, you know? I was just a few yards away from where he was lying there, dying, and I didn't even know. The store was just busy enough that I only got out to look once and I didn't see his truck, didn't even think…"

I nodded. I patted his arm. Ryan wasn't a hugger type of guy, so I didn't want to move in for too much comfort lest he take it the wrong way.

"We're up on this weird little hill," I said. "It would have been impossible for you to see the truck where it was. I didn't know him, but I was down there, just far enough back that I didn't see the accident or anything."

I didn't add that I was going to help people but did not go to Duke's truck. It had seemed that more people were helping him. I was worried about those who were less injured. I have decent first aid skills but I'm no EMT, which meant I didn't want to get in too far over my head. If Duke had died on impact, I'm glad that I hadn't been there.

I flashed on the woman in a gray sweater who been over there looking into the window, prying on the handle. She'd been driving a small blue sedan, something economical but not fancy. I wondered what she'd found or seen.

"I just feel bad. Like maybe I should have known or something."

"I'd say that's probably normal. But it's not true. You couldn't have done anything." I wanted to say more, ask more, but that felt unethical. It was one thing to casually ask about how well someone knew someone, and another to start pumping them for information, particularly during a treatment. Now, if I had been in the grocery store and Ryan started telling me, all bets were off. I just might end up there at some point.

Ryan let the subject drop, which I thought was unfortunate because he probably knew a whole lot about the family dynamics. He'd probably have known some of Duke's other friends and if he had any enemies. If it came out that Duke was murdered and it wasn't an accident, I could ask more questions. That would sound normal and just have me be an interested party.

As I finished up the treatment, I realized I was treating this as if I was an investigator and had an obligation to find the answer when I didn't actually have to. I mean Byron had the piece of paper and could enter that as evidence, and he could investigate further.

I smiled while thinking that, going back to my computer. This wasn't my mystery.

My phone rang. Byron. I picked it up foolishly thinking he was going to thank me for the piece of paper.

"This piece of paper that you think is evidence? It's a piece of garbage. Literally. It could have been by the side of the road for weeks. There's no way this points to a murder, at least not strongly enough for me to investigate it. I'd be laughed off the force for this. The paper's thin as a tissue and been scrunched up multiple times." Byron was not pleased.

"That's why I didn't give it to you immediately," I said, trying to be patient, feeling the weight of the investigation fall back on me. Duke deserved to have someone looking into his death. Even if the person who murdered him had no other reason to kill anyone ever again, taking a life should not go unpunished.

"But you did tell me," Byron said. "It fit my theory and this piece of literal garbage does nothing. Even if there's other evidence, this is a piece of garbage."

"Can't you get DNA or fingerprints from it?" I asked.

"Anyone could have touched it or bled on it or spit on it. You have no idea how long it was there. Even if it was from the murderer, it doesn't mean they wrote the thing. There's nothing to connect it to this particular case or even suggest it's about someone planning something rather than doing a creative writing exercise."

Byron was frustrated and I could appreciate it.

"I'm sorry," I said. I was. I didn't want to investigate, and I didn't want him mad at me.

"Not your fault. I should have realized when you said you picked up a paper on the side of the road."

Then I knew he was beating himself up over getting his hopes up. I felt for him. So I'd go back to doing what I could, which would be web surfing and talking to people. Cheri would be doing that down at the coffee shop, and between us, maybe we'd get enough evidence to send Byron after the killer.

I knew in my gut that there was a killer out there. I just needed to figure who it was.

Chapter 8

I worked through the afternoon seeing patients. None of my other patients offered me any information on Duke Quint. Not that I could badger my patients about people they might know the minute they came into the room. I mostly listen, and when I'm trying to solve a mystery, I might guide them just a smidge, but only a smidge. I was a healthcare provider first. I'm not even really a detective second. Maybe just an interested party second.

After my last patient was gone, I settled in to put information into the computer. I have a desktop that sits in my reception area. My work area is separated by a counter height wall covered with a piece of faux wood that's colored to match the vinyl plank I have throughout the office. It allows patients to write information down and for me to take credit cards and still keep some sort of privacy. It's a cozy little alcove, and I can just see out the main windows in the front.

I can hear the music from the back, but just barely, so it's always quiet but for the slight click of certain keys on my old black keyboard.

My massage therapist, Pam, came up to the front while she waited for her patient to get comfortable on the table. Pam is tall and slim, and she's wonderfully grounded. She knows her work as a massage therapist and she's one of the most reliable people I knew. I loved being able to bounce ideas off of her if I ran up against something unusual in my practice. I'm good. I have experience, but it's nice to be have a sounding board. It was those times when I missed my friends Lisa and Barb the most.

Lisa and Barb were both back in Vancouver, Washington, in what used to be a small town just over the river from Portland, Oregon. Vancouver has grown and it's no longer small, though I guess you'd still call it a suburb of Portland. Lisa, Barb, and I had been pals since acupuncture school. I'd started my own little clinic. Barb had joined a naturopath and worked with her. Lisa worked in her mother's chiropractic clinic. I envied both of them, having other people around. Still, we'd spent time together, bouncing ideas off of each other.

We had met once every two weeks and socialized and talked about our businesses and our clinical information. We planned out different schedules for continuing education. If we all wanted something, we might all go, but if there was something someone was only slightly interested in and another person was very interested in, we knew we'd get good feedback on the class. As more and more classes had moved online, we often took those together and kept each other honest as we watched the videos.

Now that I was back in Kentucky, I had no such support. I'd reached out to local area acupuncturists in Frankfort and Lexington, but I didn't have the same background and friendship with them that I had with Lisa and Barb. As much as I loved Cheri and appreciated being back home, there were some things I missed.

Lisa was the first person I'd ever told about my psychic abilities. She'd been a great support for me, taking it all in stride and being neither dismissive nor too overly dramatic about the potential of my abilities. She had no idea how much that was appreciated.

Pam and I didn't have that kind of bond, hadn't really had a chance to form such a thing. She also didn't know I could get impressions off items if I touched them, but she was a darned good listener. I listened to her too, particularly because she was often reporting things on mutual patients. Most of what she shared were things that could help me in my treatments, too. Pam was a bit older than I was and very motherly. Still, I never quite felt okay about telling her about my gift.

Pam had lived around the area as long as I had without my years' long break in between. I had hoped that she might know Duke Quint, but she didn't. She hadn't even seen the accident, nor had she had a chance to talk to anyone about it, at least not much. She was, unfortunately, a dead end.

I finished my computer work and logged off, ready to head home, disappointment tugging at me. I don't know what I had expected. It's not like Pam is the font of information that Cheri can be. Even if she were, it's not like she and I have the same sort of friendship.

I felt like I was running around in circles and not getting anywhere. The lack of answers nagged at me as I drove home. I wracked my brain, trying to come up with other leads. There I was, sounding all detective again. Which I am not.

I could probably talk to Daisy. She knew I'd done some investigating in the other cases. So did Morgan and Win, for that matter. Surely one of them could come up with some information from a friend of a friend. Seales is not that big.

While the day remained cool, it was beautiful. The trees were just starting to turn to gold, so there was plenty of color as I drove. Like a picture, the tulip poplars and the oaks stood behind the black split-rail fences beside the two-lane country roads that I took home. Beyond the trees and fences, driveways and farmhouses dotted the landscape. Barns were further in the distance, both the witch hat-roofed black barns and the long, low stables, always painted in a variety of colors.

Closer to Gram's, the houses got bigger, the space between them got longer, and the barns became more ornate. By the time I turned onto the driveway, I could wish I was a horse to be housed in one of those places.

Of course, I'm one to talk. Gram's house is lovely, and Byron was having my own carriage house rebuilt. I didn't actually need to be a horse, but some of those barns were pretty swanky.

I parked in the garage, which sits beyond the carriage house. The drive curves around behind, heading out towards the barn. It's not a direct walk and when it rains, it's not always pleasant, but on a day like today, it was nice. I liked the smells of the trees and the grass. The sun burned nicely, keeping me warm against the cool breeze.

Cars belonging to Daisy and Morgan shared the garage with mine—it was a long thing that held six cars. So far as I knew, the Beauvoirs had never had six cars, but perhaps my grandfather or great-grandfather was planning ahead.

I went up the few steps to the side door. Morgan got there to open it before I had a chance to use my key. He probably heard the car and was hovering until I came in.

I paused to smell the air. Win was baking something with cinnamon. She had a wonderful cinnamon twist sort of bread that she'd make to go after dinner sometimes.

"Smells wonderful," I said.

Morgan nodded.

"How was your day?" he asked.

I took off my sweater. He held the door to the coat closet. At one time he would have taken it or helped me off with it, but I'm too impatient to let someone do that for me, so we'd compromised. I let him hold the door while I hung up my own clothing.

As much as I liked being part of a family of sorts here in the big house, I really would like being out in the carriage house where I didn't have someone doing things for me that I felt I should do myself.

"I'll make you some tea," Morgan said. I'd purchased some loose-leaf herbal tea that I liked and taken to having a cup when I got home in the afternoon.

"Thanks," I said. Again, it was something I could do, but Morgan and Win seemed to think it was their job to do that.

I took my stuff upstairs to put away. I'd change into sweats and lounge around the house. I doubted I'd be seeing Byron. He had planned to work on the carriage house that evening, but I had a feeling this investigation might keep him away. If not that, then his own frustration at thinking it was more than an accident and not being able to prove it would do so. I had found that Byron was very good at stewing about frustrations alone.

I sighed. I hated it that he was mad at me. I had known he would be. The paper really wasn't much of a clue, but I knew what I had felt. My gut told me I was right to connect it to the so-called accident. Too bad Byron couldn't use that with his boss.

I was just coming out of my room when Daisy hurried down the hall from the stairs. She was still in riding boots and flared pants. Her face was pink with the wind, so she'd clearly taken Blackjax out for a good run.

"Nice ride?" I asked.

"Perfect," she said.

I smiled and headed downstairs for my tea. Win bustled around the kitchen while I played on my phone, reading up on what had happened during the day on the news sites. Then I allowed myself to browse my social media. Cheri had posted a photo of her and Travis out on a country road buying apple cider.

I had to laugh. Cider is not Cheri's drink of choice, but Travis enjoyed searching out little roadway stands to find farm-fresh goods. It wasn't that he was a foodie, really, he more enjoyed the find and talking to the folks who ran those places.

"How was your day?" Daisy asked, coming down. Her hair was still damp from a shower, and she was in black leggings and a soft pink V-neck tunic top.

"Good," I said. "No accidents this evening."

"That was just horrible," Daisy said quietly. "I don't know what gets into people now. Everyone is always in a hurry to get somewhere. No one really realizes what they have, do they?"

I shook my head.

Daisy sighed. "I remember Mr. Kelley. Marty had him for social sciences. Did you?"

I nodded. "He was a nice enough, but a little creepy. I thought he was going to retire out of the area."

"Didn't work out," Daisy said, confirming Cheri's gossip. "And Marty didn't like him too much either. I'm not even sure she would have given him the 'nice enough' comment."

"What about Duke Quint?" I asked. "I think he was a bit older than me, so I didn't know him."

"He was a year behind Marty, I think," Daisy said. "He was in a couple of her classes. Smart boy, if I recall correctly. Nice. His sister was quite the partier. Even Marty heard about that though the sister was several grades ahead. Too bad. Duke's father must be devastated."

I noticed Daisy didn't mention knowing how he felt. Certainly her loss of Marty was different from Bud Quint's loss of his son, but both were sudden and unexpected losses.

"It was a weird accident," I said, feeling out what my aunt might have heard.

"My mama heard it wasn't an accident," Win said as she took out the cinnamon twists from the oven and covered them to let them cool enough to drizzle with frosting.

"I hadn't heard anything official," I said. "I know that Byron was interviewing folks to make sure everything checked out. He seemed like he might have thought there was more to it than an accident." There, that was politic, wasn't it? Just making sure.

Win shook her head. "Someone reported that the white truck that forced the black truck to run into the ditch, across all the lanes of traffic, was found abandoned in Frankfort. Reported stolen. And no one is saying that the semi almost hit it. It just crossed in front the truck and seemed like it deliberately tried to force Duke's truck off the road."

"How did they know the truck they found was the same truck? Surely there are plenty of white trucks." I said.

"Traffic cameras. An older couple who was injured had one on their dash and caught the truck on camera. The police have it now."

That should have made Byron happy. I wondered if he'd found that out before or after he'd called to yell at me about a piece of garbage.

"When did you hear this?" I sipped my tea. I was itching to grab one of the twists, but Win would slap my hand if I did. Besides, they were better with frosting.

"Maybe a half an hour ago?" Win said. "Mama called and let me know. Duke Quint used to come by and tutor my brother in math."

"Everything I've heard about him says he was a nice guy," I said. "Who would want him dead?"

Win shrugged. "Isn't that for your boyfriend to find out?"

"Well, someone went to a lot of trouble to make things look like an accident," I said. "He could probably use all the leads he can get. Has your brother talked to him?"

Win let her head fall to her shoulder and gave me a look. Her family was Mexican, and while they were legal, they avoided law enforcement whenever they could. It hadn't been helped when Win had been taken in for questioning about Marty's murder. She'd hadn't had anything to do with it, but all the same, it hadn't helped her distrust of the police—or her family's.

"Okay, so I'm asking you in case you know something you don't know you know." I waited for Win to speak, to see what she might know.

She sighed, putting a hand on her hip. "Okay." Finally. She moved to the table and put her hands on it, leaning on it, as if she needed strength. I wondered what was so hard about talking about Duke Quint.

"Duke was a nice guy. He didn't charge us to tutor my brother, even. I mean, he got something out of it. He put it on his college application. He was kind of sneaky, though, you know? I caught him looking at me when I changed clothes, when the door should have been closed tight—I thought I had, but maybe…"

I nodded.

Win went on. "It happened twice. After that I never changed clothes while he was there. Never went to the bathroom, even though that door had a lock. I didn't trust him. He never touched me, never acted badly or sent out pictures or anything like that. He was just kind of creepy in a low-level way."

"So he could have been looking by accident," I said.

Win nodded.

There was that phrase again, make it look like an accident. Had Duke done something "by accident" on purpose and this was payback? Had the person even meant to kill him?

"Anything else?"

"Just that he never came by once he went off to school. I mean no one expected him to. He was polite, smart, knew his stuff, but we weren't friendly, really."

Win went back to the kitchen and started putting frosting on the twists.

Talking to her had given me my first opening into why someone might have wanted to hurt Duke Quint. Had he finally gone too far?

Chapter 9

Win made us her mother's version of arroz con pollo for dinner. I have to say it's far better than anything you can find in a restaurant, particularly here in Kentucky. It smelled good and would go wonderfully with the cinnamon twists. Win and Morgan wouldn't eat with Daisy and I, though we often tried to persuade them. They stayed out of our way while we ate in the kitchen, but with ears always alert for anything we might need, though both of us were quite able-bodied and could stand up and move to the kitchen to get it.

"I don't like what we just heard about Duke," Daisy said. "I mean, I didn't know him really, nor did Marty, but to think what he did to Win and at such a young age…"

I nodded as I ate. I hated to think about murder with such good food. The chicken was perfectly tender and moist, and the spices were perfect. They were probably a bit much for the average Seales' palate, but I'd eaten Mexican food around the country. I preferred mine with a healthy dose of spice. Daisy appeared to have no problem with it either.

"I wonder if Byron's heard this? I mean, it doesn't sound like something someone would murder over, but it's sure possible Duke graduated to doing something worse. I mean, he was young when he'd watch Win and then try and make it like she was imagining it. What else could he be pretending to not do?"

"Gaslighting," Daisy said. "You hear about it all the time now, and maybe he did something like that. But you push someone too far, and they won't take it any longer."

We appeared to be on the same wavelength, at least as far as Duke was concerned.

Talk turned to other things, like the horses and life around the property in general. We finished eating, both of us plenty full, though we made sure there was enough room for a cinnamon twist.

Byron called while Win was serving us up one of those.

"I wanted to apologize for how I acted earlier. This is a bizarre case. I knew there was something wrong and I just wanted some proof. That piece of paper just wasn't it. Fortunately, people are getting dash cams and one of those showed what happened. Looks deliberate, though even if we catch the driver, it's likely they'll say it was an accident, but now we have some leverage. I shouldn't have taken my frustration out on you."

"It's okay," I said. "I told you the paper wasn't much."

"I wanted it to be something," Byron said. "I wish it were. I mean the dash cam is enough to investigate, but it's not definitive proof. A smoking gun like that paper would be wonderful. It's just so old and worn that there's no way to be certain how long it's been there."

We chatted a bit before he rang off. He was heading into Lexington to talk to a couple of Duke's friends to get a better sense of Duke's life. Byron had waited to clear it with local police so they wouldn't be surprised. Certainly the Seales police force could have asked people to come here, but it was less intrusive to folks to have someone come to their house. Or maybe not. Maybe it was more intrusive and that was the whole point.

While the dash cam helped bolster my feelings, so much still relied on that note. If I'd left it by the side of road, would that have been better? At least Byron could have proved it didn't come from my garbage. But who knew it would become a clue, a real clue, rather than just someone angry?

I shuttered that thought aside. With all the wind, it could have blown anywhere, and after the accident it was certainly possible that it would have been tossed away, and no one would have seen it then either.

I put a piece of cinnamon twist in my mouth and chewed. The flavors of sweet icing and the spicy cinnamon burst forth. It was a heavenly finish to the spicier dinner we'd had. Win was a marvelous cook. Gram had been lucky to find her.

"I'm going to call your mom," Daisy said. "If I remember correctly, she worked at the school when Duke was there. I'm sure she'd appreciate being able to chat about it."

I nodded. "If she doesn't know anything, maybe Chelsea could dig something up."

Daisy looked confused.

"My friend Erik's wife?" I didn't add that she'd been at Marty's funeral and that was the only place Daisy was likely to have met her.

"If she's your age, she's probably too young to know much," Daisy said. "Your mom will remember something, I'm sure."

I let Daisy head off to call without volunteering to do so myself. First, my mom and I struggle a bit with our relationship. She disapproves my psychic abilities and finds them sort of offensive, though I'm not certain why. She'd been the one to convince me never to tell anyone. She'd been horrified to find out that I'd helped Elle Mabry by touching something and giving her a reading. It had been too much to hope that my mom wouldn't hear about that.

Despite that little rift, my mom and I get along okay. Maybe not as well as Cheri and her mom, but well enough.

Daisy was practically my mom's best friend, though, so I was certain she was likely to hear more than I would.

My aunt may only have been my mother's sister-in-law, but the two got along famously. Mom had been the one to comfort her when Marty had died. I had a feeling that if my mom was at all upset about the death of Duke Quint, Daisy would be the one to offer her comfort.

Besides, my mom disapproved of my getting involved in all these murders. I'd heard about it after they caught Jaci. If I'd been living at home, I'd have been grounded. Fortunately, it's hard to ground an adult.

As I started thinking of all the other things my mom disapproved of, like me going off to Portland to study acupuncture, I realized my mom seemed to enjoy disapproving of me living my life. It was an interesting insight. Fortunately, I had always had Gram to support me and tell me whatever I was doing was great. It had never occurred to me that I was missing anything from my mother. Maybe that's why losing Gram had been so difficult.

I heard a car drive up outside as I stood, thinking about whether I wanted to go upstairs to do some accounting work or if I wanted to settle in and watch a bit of television, seeing Byron wasn't available.

I went to the side door and looked out.

"Thad?" I said.

Thad was a friend from my time at the University of Kentucky. He'd stayed around here and gotten a job as an enrichment advisor for a small aerospace company that was just northeast of Lexington. He didn't get out to Seales all that often. Just dropping in was more than a little unusual.

"I caught you!" he said. "I was on my way back from a meeting in Louisville and thought I'd drop by."

"Great," I said. "I just finished dinner, but Win made some wonderful cinnamon twists, if you'd like one?"

Thad made a face and then let his hands go down his body. He's funny that way. "I wouldn't want to mess with perfection. I had greens and healthy stuff this evening, and I can't possibly ruin it."

He sauntered across the driveway and followed me inside.

"Tea or coffee?" I asked.

Thad shook his head.

"Something harder?"

"Sadly, I have to drive and can't stay long enough to enjoy it." He settled on the sofa in the great room, flopping down as if he owned the place. Thad could be uptight sometimes, but at other times he took over.

"So if you can't stay, what brings you here?" I waited, thinking he had some sort of favor he wanted to ask. Did he need money? A place to house a horse? Advice on some embarrassing health problem? Maybe even a cheap place to throw one of his enrichment parties?

"Duke Quint," Thad said.

"You knew him?" Thad wasn't from Seales, so a connection surprised me.

"Lucas, my current squeeze, knew him. And he's devastated. He knows no one here in Seales, and I guess he's supposed to talk to the police. He's more than a little worried that your people will see a gay man and decide he did it." Thad shrugged like that was the furthest thing from his mind.

"I know the detective who's going to see him. Byron Cabot. You remember him from Marty's death?" Thad had been peripherally around when

Marty had died. We'd talked about Byron, and he'd encouraged me in the relationship. Of course, everyone had, so perhaps that wasn't exactly saying he was unique.

"The cute boy who liked you," Thad said.

"He's interviewing Lucas, so I don't think you have to worry unless Lucas actually did something."

Thad made a face. "Sometimes I wonder."

"Why?" I asked, leaning back, trying to be casual.

"Lucas was always mad at Duke. Duke liked to think he was straight and went out with a bunch of different women. Lucas was sure Duke was just lying to himself."

"What did you think?" I wanted a non-lovelorn take on Duke.

Thad shrugged. "Maybe? But I doubt it. I think the only thing that made me think Lucas might be onto something was the fact that Duke was always trying too hard with the women. He was a good-looking man. He could have had anyone, but he was kept pushing, you know? Like he had something to prove."

I nodded. I filed that away, though I doubted that being a closeted gay man would get him killed. Except maybe by a girlfriend who was angry with him. Of course, a girl could be obsessed with him if he was seeing other women too. It didn't have to be a man.

"Anyway, he and Lucas were pals even though I thought Lucas picked at him a bit much. Fortunately, it's not serious between us, otherwise I'd have been jealous. At least I'm not serious. I just got out of a relationship and I'm not really ready for something serious. Neither is Lucas."

"So are you here to just check out the cop who will be talking to Lucas, or did you have more?" I asked.

"Lucas said Duke was acting odd the last few days. Not enough to say something or put a finger on anything. But Duke was acting like he thought things were going to change. Lucas talked about it a little, and we're both trying to figure out what it could have been. Duke might have been kind of a dog when it came to women, but he wasn't a bad guy. He had a good job, lived within his means so far as we could see, didn't seem to be into drugs or anything that would have given him a ton of debt, you know. So what was going to change was hard to say." Thad leaned back. "Maybe I should have had that drink."

"Why?" I asked.

"I hate this," Thad said. "I just hate this. I hate talking about someone that Lucas is in love with, and that if he stays with me, it's because I'm left over."

"I thought you weren't serious?" I was used to Thad's swinging emotions, but he'd usually be solid about the whole relationship thing.

"It's supposed to not be serious. I didn't even want to be serious, but maybe the fact that Lucas really isn't serious and probably is in love with someone else has hooked me. I'm such a mess." Thad laughed a little.

"Nah," I said. "You're Thad. And you're always something of a mess. I can't believe you'd fall for a guy hung up on someone else."

"I know, right?!" Thad practically jumped out of his seat. "Especially a guy probably hung up on a straight guy. And now he's not even a living guy, and there's no way to live up to that."

I smiled a little.

"I told him I'd see what I could find out in Seales. I figured Seales is small enough that I was hoping you might have heard something…" Thad gave me his big puppy dog eyes. They were something of a joke between us, but they also worked.

I laughed and then said. "Well, I was there. I mean not to help Duke, but I was coming out of work when it happened. I was just far enough back that I didn't get injured or anything. I did go out and help some of the folks who got rear-ended when everyone slammed on their brakes. I know that Byron is looking into it, making sure it's really an accident and all that."

"What do you mean?" Thad sat up straight and leaned forward.

"Just that. He has to rule out anything other than an accident before closing the books. It was a huge mess here." I hoped I hadn't said too much. I love Thad to death, but he can be a gossip.

"But is there any reason to think it wasn't?" Thad asked.

I reached out to touch his hand, a hand wearing a ring. I let myself open just a bit, hoping that I wouldn't go under too much of a trance from the ring. Thad was just a little too interested in this. While I couldn't see him as part of a murder plot, he could be a game player. A small voice suggested that was exactly what Duke was. Which might be why Lucas was attracted to both men.

I felt lots of pride from the ring. Worry. Thad was always worried. I saw a series of men and flirtations. I got a close vision of a tall blond man, soul patch under his chin, smiling a little, holding a hard cider. The name Sean came to mind, but I couldn't be certain. He'd been important, far more important than Lucas. I got a sense of a connection to Lucas but that was all.

I drew myself back. The ring wasn't as important to Thad as I had hoped. No major emotions with it. I wondered who Sean was.

"I think someone saw something that made

them think the driver of the car that caused it swerved for no reason," I said. That way I wasn't lying but I also wasn't making it sound too much like it could have been deliberate. "That's all I know."

Thad nodded. I left out the rest. I hated not trusting one of my oldest friends, but if the last year had taught me anything, it was that old friends weren't always what they could have been.

Thad's phone rang. He answered it without even looking at me. He seemed lost in thought.

"I'll be right there," he said.

I raised an eyebrow. "Lucas. He doesn't want to be alone when he talks to the police. I guess your guy is there. Want to come along?"

I could just imagine what Byron would say if I marched in there after someone had kept him waiting. Though it was tempting to hear what Lucas had to say, I wasn't going to go ruining my relationship just because I was nosy.

"That's okay," I told Thad. "Call me if you need me."

Thad nodded and left. I watched him go, the easy way he drove in his older model gray sedan. There was a scratch on the door. I felt as if I'd seen that before. I told myself I was being silly. There was no way Thad could have been at the scene of the accident, and even if he was, why not say so?

Chapter 10

The next day I got up and went to work. It was a glorious morning with blue skies and just a hint of crisp cool air. It had the slightest smell of rain in the air and darker clouds were rolling in from the west. At this angle, they might go north, but I couldn't count on it.

My morning stayed equally pleasant. I talked to patients but no one knew anything more. They were more than eager to gossip. It sounded like most people believed that the accident wasn't really an accident. Most people thought that Duke had been murdered. That's the problem with a small town. Gossip runs rampant. At this point, even if it did turn out to be an accident, not that I believed it was, no one else would believe it either. As for theories, I head everything from an old girlfriend to secret FBI or NSA conspiracies.

I tended to think that Duke Quint, who worked as a low-level engineer, would not be interesting enough for the FBI or NSA. The engineering firm he worked on was making parts for an aerospace firm. While they might have done some work for the government, I had a hard time believing whatever small part they made was so important that Duke would be selling state secrets somewhere.

Pam wasn't in that day, so I had the place to myself. Lunch came and went, and pretty soon I was heading out to the coffee shop where I was meeting Cheri. We'd agreed to go into Lexington for some shopping and then maybe a movie.

I parked along the street downtown. There was plenty of parking downtown that afternoon. It can get bad when court is in session and people use the street parking for when the courthouse parking gets full. Sometimes City Hall gets busy, too, and their lot gets full. That wasn't the case today.

I got a space only two spaces down from the coffee shop where Cheri worked. I had to wait for a few cars to pass before I could get out and open my door. I was standing on the sidewalk about to walk up to the door, smelling the exhaust of the car that just passed coughing out smoke, when Cheri rushed out. She had on a heavy black sweater that came down almost to her knees. It flapped around over a body-hugging round neck, long sleeved t-shirt, and black jeans. She had on ballet slippers for shoes and that was it.

"I saw you go past," Cheri said, "and I grabbed my stuff and ran—you would not believe how busy we've been today!"

"What's going on?" I asked, putting the car back in gear and signaling to go out into traffic. The air was still smelling of exhaust and I closed the vent on the car. I'd need to put on the air conditioning if it didn't clear soon. The clouds had passed us to the north, as I thought they might, and bright sun kept the car warm, particularly with the dark interior. Outside the temperature might require sweaters and jackets, but inside the car it was quite toasty.

I was in a light turtleneck with a sweatshirt over it. I'd pulled the sweatshirt on after leaving work. I work in casual clothing, but a UK sweatshirt seemed a bit too casual.

"I have no idea," Cheri said, pulling her sweater around her and settling in while I pulled out into traffic. I turned the music down, though it still played low in the background. "Although everyone is gossiping about Duke Quint. I heard one woman saying she thought he might have been killed by the same people who got Jeffrey Epstein."

"That's a new one," I said. "I've heard some good conspiracy stories, though, too. Did the woman who thought whoever killed him also killed Epstein have any proof that Duke might have been into procuring young women in his spare time?"

"No," Cheri said, a bit too seriously I thought. "I think he's supposed to just have liked young women. I don't know about *that,* but there are several reports that he's quite a ladies' man, and not always nice about it. He just ghosts women he's been with. Ghosting's not uncommon, you know, and I mean, it happens, but I can't see someone getting so mad that they'd kill him."

"That was what I was thinking."

"I haven't heard anything about his work or something like that," Cheri said. "It's just an engineering firm even though I'm sure I heard some of those conspiracy theories too. I talked to Ayla, the manager, and she has a cousin who works at the same place—not in engineering but in human resources—and she says they don't even work for the government at this particular plant. They have an office in Virginia that does the government work and so far as she knows, Duke never goes there!"

"I looked them up and I figured that they

didn't seem like they made anything that would be super secretive, at least not from their website. I guess a website wouldn't say that though, right?" I laughed at myself.

"They make parts for small planes. I forget exactly what the parts are, but it's not like something anyone would kill someone over or blackmail them into getting plans for," Cheri said. "But that's what we've been hearing. Ayla has been laughing every time someone brings that up. Hopefully her laughing will shut down that line of gossip and we'll start getting something good—and by good, I mean true."

I turned left onto the main highway out of town. "Highway" used to mean a heavily traveled road, but in this part of Kentucky it was often just the main road going to or from a city. This was a two-lane country road which, for the moment, was lined with black split rail fences—because around here everything is—and trees and even some low bushes. In the distance I saw a water tower over the top of a horse barn in browns and greens.

Soon enough, I'd come to the junction with Highway 60, which we'd take into Lexington and the traffic there, though to me, even at rush hour, traffic never seemed particularly bad. It's why I was driving and not Cheri. She found Lexington traffic a bit much. Fortunately, she'd never visited me when I lived just outside Portland, Oregon, and so she'd never had to deal with "real" traffic.

"Everything I've been listening to says that people kind of liked him. I mean he did nice things, but then there's this undertone of smarmy about him, you know? Like he's one person to some people and another to others," Cheri said. "You don't suppose he has a multiple personality disorder or something, you know like that woman in the old movie?"

I smiled a little as I signaled to turn onto Highway 60. Cheri's mom was a huge fan of old movies, and no doubt there was one about a woman with multiple personalities. I'd not been a big fan of old movies, though both Cheri and I watched many of them over at her house growing up. The DVD collection was filled with them. I didn't recall one in particular, but it's possible we watched it and I just hadn't paid that much attention.

"I think multiple personality disorder isn't as common as movies make us think," I said, remembering something I had read in school. I had an interest in psychology as well as acupuncture, so I'd done a lot of reading about things like that.

Cheri shrugged it off. "Still, if he was kind of a jerk to some people, maybe he was a jerk to the wrong person."

"Which is likely, given he's dead," I said.

That made Cheri chuckle a little and then she silenced herself. "I shouldn't laugh at a dead man. I guess you are right. And I mean, who can know? Even with all those people liking him, we all liked Jaci and look what happened with her."

Cheri was referring to the fact that last spring my barn manager had turned out to be running drugs for extra money. She wasn't doing it through the farm until one of her middlemen was killed. That ended up requiring her to hold drugs on the property and have someone pick them up. I found out and she'd held me at gun point, but fortunately the police were already onto her. Still, the idea of having a gun pointed at me again made my stomach knot while my body grew cold.

I'd done a lot of needling on myself and even gone to another practitioner to help work through it. I figured I had worked through it enough mentally that I just needed to get it out of my body. I was probably going to have to come to terms with the fact that it would always be there, always be an experience that was a part of me, just like Marty's death was a part of me, but I wanted to forget about that gun and the terror that had taken over for a moment.

"True," I said. "It seems like we just haven't talked to the right people. Maybe his friends in Lexington would know more? I think Byron was going to talk to some folks yesterday."

"You haven't already talked to him?" Cheri asked.

"I was going to later on.. Aunt Daisy was going to see what my mom knew. I guess she worked at the school while Duke was there, and Daisy was going to pump her for information."

"Maybe she'll find out why they named him Duke," Cheri said. "I mean let's be real. Who names their child Duke? Even if we do live in Kentucky, there ought to be some limit on what you can name your child. It's ridiculous."

That made me laugh.

"You're funny."

"Still, I can't wait to hear what you hear from Byron," Cheri said.

I paid attention to the road while Cheri continued talking.

"I heard about this guy Sean in Lexington who knew Duke. The rumors, and this comes from one of the people who were talking about the stupid stuff about Duke's death being a conspiracy, said that Sean was gay and that Duke sort of led him on purposely. There was another guy there, Lucas or something, and they said the two were working out how to pay him back for that," Cheri said while we passed Bluegrass airport just as a small plane was about to land.

"Death seems extreme for leading them on," I said. Thad had talked about Lucas.

"I know," Cheri said. "I didn't say I believed it, but I figured if those names come up for Byron, you'll know to pay attention because they actually knew Duke and everything."

"I wonder if he didn't lead them on romantically," I said.

"What?"

I told her what Thad had said. And also what Win had said. Cheri and I agreed that while Duke sounded like kind of a jerk, those weren't things that people normally got murdered over.

"What if it was a business thing? Like Duke was going to do something for someone for a business or something, but he overpromised and then tried to smarm his way out of it?" I didn't know where that came from. Maybe Cheri's general commentary had me putting something together.

"Money is always a big motivator and I could see someone killing over that, but you have to ask why someone would hire Duke for something? He has a job already."

"He's an engineer. Maybe they needed him to design something?" I suggested. I had no real idea. That didn't quite fit. Duke had other talents. I just didn't know what they were.

Chapter 11

After a satisfying evening shopping and a movie, I got home late and climbed into bed. It was a good break from thinking about Duke Quint and the murders. I felt almost normal. Young again, even, considering I was wandering around a mall in a way I hadn't in years.

I probably looked tired coming down to breakfast. I was regretting agreeing to see a movie with Cheri after shopping. I had patients and I needed to be awake. I was going to need a large cup of coffee.

"You were out late last night," Daisy said, probably noticing that I was moving more slowly than usual.

She was at the round table near the kitchen, in

her usual spot, wrapped in a blue and green floral robe of the sort I didn't realize they still made. It was probably polyester and cotton rather than silk. Daisy won't spend a ton of money on clothing, preferring to have more rather than good quality.

Her hair was combed, though, and I noticed she'd managed to put on a bit of makeup.

"Cheri and I went shopping and then to a movie. I don't think either of us expected to shop for so long." Which was true. We'd only been looking for shoes, but then we'd spotted a few other things. I know we'd both considered leaving after eating, but the theater was so close that we'd decided to stay late.

That segued into a discussion of the movie and whether Daisy wanted to see it or not.

"I was hoping to tell you what I learned from your mother," she said as she finished her omelet. I was just onto bacon at that point. I don't have it often but when I did, I always made sure to enjoy it. Win had gotten the thick sliced strips of pepper bacon which I loved.

"What?" I asked, leaning forward. Putting it like that, I hoped that my mom had actually had some insight from her job.

"She remembered Duke, of course. Everyone had been talking about him, so it was easy to bring it up. I didn't even have to mention that you were involved in any way. I even avoided the accident, so she didn't know you were there then either. I figured if you wanted to tell her, you could."

Which was nice of her. My mom would freak if she knew I'd nearly been in an accident. She worries. She'd gotten worse after Marty died, as if Daisy losing a child had brought a reality home to her that she hadn't really thought about. I may be frustrated with my mother, and we might not always see eye to eye, but she does love her children.

"I think she thinks that if you do know anything, it's just because of Byron, so it's easy to avoid mention of your impressions. I do wish your mother wasn't so adamant that it's weird to have psychic abilities." Daisy looked away, making a little face.

I smiled.

Babs came into the kitchen and made a little mew, staring at Daisy.

"Oh, dear. Win, are they out of food?" Daisy started to stand up, but Win waved her off, going to the pantry to get something just in case. That brought Hellspark running from upstairs. He made his way downstairs, the stiff-legged run he'd started within the last year or so as arthritis began to set in. I ought to work with him, but he was reluctant to be messed with. His stiffness didn't keep him from anything he really wanted.

"You were saying?" I prompted when the two

cats had had their food dish topped off. I'm a big fan of cats, so when I say they were never out of food, I am not just being unkind. Everyone in the house was willing to top the dish off without looking. The two were fed canned food when Morgan got up with first light and usually shortly before we sat down to dinner, also by Morgan. Everyone else just dropped some crunchies in a dish.

"Duke was known to the office where your mom worked and not just because he was a student. Naturally, they know all their students. The teachers all said that Duke had a tendency to fly under the radar, if you know what I mean. They'd be certain he had a part in some prank or other that got another child in trouble, but no one could ever prove he was involved. I guess his first-grade teacher caught him a couple of times, but after that he was sneaky as heck."

"Interesting," I said.

"In fact, his second-grade teacher would always argue that he'd been perfectly nice in her class. Always one to volunteer to help, always nice to the other kids. Said he never got out of hand at all. I think she had to scold him a few times, as everyone does with kids, but overall a really well-behaved child. She was unusual. The other teachers always sort of knew he was into things."

"So he gets others in trouble for what he

does," I said. If he was always setting up others, perhaps he'd set up a scheme that went wrong. Someone could have lost a job, or worse.

"That's what it sounds like," Daisy said. "What do you suppose he could have done to get someone to murder him? And in a way that made it look like an accident?"

"I suppose it depends upon the person. But you have to realize that the car accident, if it was the person in the truck, didn't just kill Duke. It also killed Mr. Ellis and injured a number of other people. It basically destroyed the semi."

Daisy nodded. "Poor Mr. Ellis. So many people were talking about him, too, though everyone thinks it was Duke who was the target. Mr. Ellis was just unlucky. Did you know that he was on his way to the airport when it happened? He was planning to fly to Atlanta to meet his wife and see his kids."

"I knew that the kids lived there," I said. "I didn't realize he was going to see them."

Another nod as Daisy set down her fork. "I guess his wife was already there. She'd left the week before, but Mr. Ellis got called for jury duty. He could have put it off, but he said he just wanted to get it over with."

I shook my head.

"Originally he and his wife were going to

drive. I guess the gossips say he didn't really want to have to drive with her. She's a very nervous rider, so he got her a plane ticket and then was going to drive himself. His son gave him the plane ticket so that he could get there sooner."

Which was a really sad story when you thought about it.

"How horrible for his family," I said.

"I know," Daisy told me. "And imagine, whoever started it couldn't have been sure that Duke was dead."

I nodded. It was a very imprecise way of murdering someone, not to mention what happened to other people. Duke could have just gone off the road and not died.

"I haven't heard any gossip about how exactly Duke died. I mean he could have just run off the road. He was in a truck, for heaven's sake!" I suppose I'm slow for just realizing that, but I'm not an expert on how people die.

"Your mom heard that his seatbelt didn't latch quite right and flew off when he hit. His airbag didn't deploy either. I expect that's what allowed Byron to start investigating this as more than an accident. Either one of the things would have been bad luck, but both? Plus, it looked like the truck had low brake fluid and issues with the steering even though it was practically new. Any sort of accident would have probably caused him a great deal of injury, if not death."

"Someone knew cars, then," I said. "They knew how to fix the car. But if he lost his brakes, why not just let him go without causing an accident? No, never mind. Flat land. I'm used to more hilly areas."

Daisy nodded. "Even on most of our hills it wouldn't have been bad. A couple of places in Frankfort, but there was no indication he went there very often."

"So why here?" I finished my food and settled back. I needed to leave soon, but Daisy was helping me figure some stuff out. "What was here that made them decide to let him die here? Was it just opportunity, or was there some reason he had to die at that intersection? He lives in Lexington but the accident happened here. I mean, it would have been just as easy to cause an accident there, right?"

Daisy gave me a long look. Penelope Blue popped in and pretended to rub her cold body against my lower legs. I couldn't feel her exactly, but my shins got chilled and achy.

"I can't imagine what it was," Daisy said.

"Maybe that's something I ought to ask Cheri. Or you could ask my mom. Or we could both go around asking folks things," I said. "I mean, what's there?"

"The grocery store, your office, the other buildings around your office." Daisy started listing them off.

I mentally went through names of people that I knew there. No one jumped out as having ties to Duke Quint. When Layla Wiltshire had been found dead outside my office last spring, there had been too many suspects. With Duke, there were too few, or rather, they all seemed to be hiding under rocks.

Layla had been placed there after being killed elsewhere. Duke had just been killed down below the office. It seemed like this wasn't exactly a lucky corner. I ought to have someone come in and do some sort of energetic clearing on my office. I mean, I didn't want to be next. That would wait, though.

It seemed that the person who wanted Duke dead also wanted to be sneaky. Was it just to not get caught, or was it for another reason? Perhaps what they saw as poetic justice?

The thought hit me that perhaps there was a reason they wanted to kill him and make it look like a car accident. As I said my goodbyes to Daisy and grabbed my stuff, my head was filled with the idea that perhaps Duke had caused someone else to cause an accident, perhaps someone who lived or worked near the intersection where he had died.

My gut said it felt right. The fact that Penelope Blue followed me out of the house, making little meow moves made me think I was on the right track.

Chapter 12

Work took up most of the day. People were still talking about the accident, particularly those who hadn't been out to this intersection since it had happened. I had a feeling this was going to be the main topic of conversation for some time—at least until something more gossip-worthy came along. Which is a sad statement on humanity as far as I'm concerned.

I listened for any new clues about the accident. Mostly I was hoping someone might remember something else significant happening at this intersection. Maybe Duke had been involved. He was older than I was, so maybe I had been too young to pay attention. I could see someone thinking that it was poetic justice to have him die there.

I pictured the intersection from when I was younger. The feed store had been over on the other side of the road, and the big parking lot where my clinic was had been an old used car lot. It wasn't the nice kind that typically sprang up around all the other car dealerships, but rather the old sort where you picked up a junker when you couldn't afford anything better.

My dad had brought me there to look for my first car. We hadn't found anything he and I could agree on—me about style and him about what was under the hood. We'd ended purchasing from a used car dealer in Lexington that had something a bit better for only a few hundred dollars more. We'd taken so long to find a car, I'd had time to save that extra money while hunting around, too.

I recalled the gas station, which sat a few blocks up, had always been there. It was convenient for when you were heading out of town, through Frankfort and then on to Louisville. Going the other way, the best gas stations were down in Versailles. There were three there that always had the lowest prices. If I'd been thinking, I would have filled up when Cheri and I drove through the town when we came back from Lexington.

While needling my patients, I made myself focus on them. Acupuncture is so much about intent that I needed to be present. That didn't mean my mind wasn't off in a million different directions the moment I closed the door.

I wanted to go searching for more information on any deaths in this area, but I didn't get a chance to. I had two new patients in addition to a full day of return patients. New patients always make me more tired. I was more than ready to close up by the end of the day. It had been a long day and an even longer week.

The smell of pizza outside in the parking lot was heavenly, reminding me I hadn't eaten nearly enough at lunch. I wondered what Win and Morgan would say if I came in with giant pizza with the works. I waved at Deena, the woman who runs the pizza place as I stood on the sidewalk thinking.

Deena gestured to me to come in. While all hands were busy tossing pepperoni or sausage on well-sauced pies or else answering phones, there weren't any other customers waiting. I saw one of Deena's drivers collecting boxes to take out for delivery.

"Did you get stuck out in that traffic the other night?" Deena asked.

"Yep," I said. "Probably gave you a bit of business though. People coming in while they were waiting."

"I wish," Deena said. "Mostly it was people mad because our delivery driver had to detour around and it took him longer. I think the people pulling out were going to the grocery store or turning around so they could hit up the bar over on Elkhorn."

The bar out on Elkhorn used to be a kind of locals only hangout. It looked like a brick prison chamber from the outside, the windows small and narrow with a solid wood door. The sign on the building was small and hard to read unless you were standing right under it in daylight. The flashing Bud sign was the only indication that it was actually a bar.

They made good wings, and if you were in the mood, that was the place to go. They were also known for pouring a pretty strong drink, which meant their mixers were expensive, though they kept their tap beer prices low. There was one television, not very big, for the whole place. Still, the bar did a good enough business that it was usually tough to find a table. Years after being forced to go non-smoking, it still smelled like cigarette smoke and probably would until the building itself was torn down.

Wings actually sounded good. I'd have to mention that to Win. She had a recipe—she does for pretty much anything unless it's Asian food—

that was to die for. She'd make some for me if I asked. Byron would like that, too, so I'd have to tell him to drop by for dinner even if he was too busy to work on the carriage house.

"Too bad," I said. "I'd have thought you were swamped."

"Got a few. Just not as many as I'd have liked," Deena winked. Which meant they had been swamped but lots of folks went elsewhere.

I nodded and sniffed the air. She was making garlic breadsticks as well. Now I wanted those, too. Clearly I was hungry enough that almost anything would taste good.

"I'll make you up a box of breadsticks," Deena said, reading my mind. "Small or large?"

"Small. It's probably just me and Daisy." I watched the kids making pizzas.

Deena nodded. "You know, Duke worked for me back in the day when I was downtown."

Before the grocery store and surrounding buildings had been built, Deena had run the pizza place out of one of the old buildings downtown. I remembered trying to find parking on the street on popular nights. You could cruise up and down looking for a place close. Mostly I ended up parking in the courthouse lot a few blocks away.

"Really?" I asked.

Deena nodded. "Lasted about three months.

Seemed like a nice kid except the till was always off while he was here. Never gave me reason to blame him except it started coming out right just after he left. And when I say off, I mean short. Always. Mistakes happen and some kids just aren't good counters, but they're over as often as they're short, you know?"

I nodded. So another person who had something to say about Duke.

"Can't imagine that a few bucks would have made someone murder him. And you'd think if it was the company he worked for, they'd have charged him with something. That's illegal, ain't it? Never mind. It is. I know that. I might be a Kentucky redneck, but I'm not an idiot."

I laughed. Deena is no one's idiot and she's not your typical redneck. She might run a pizza joint, but she went to Ohio State and studied physics. She'd considered getting her doctorate, but her mom fell off a ladder. Deena came back that summer to help out. She'd ended up working in the pizza place around the corner from her house. She found she liked working with her hands, baking pizzas, and then delivering them. She had some ideas for new flavors, taken from what people ordered, and ended up buying the place when Old Man Porter decided to retire.

She'd moved locations twice since then, and

this was probably the most successful, though she was trying to decide if she wanted to open a second location down in Versailles or up in Frankfort.

"Bad way to die, though," I said, thinking of the accident.

"Especially as a murder. I mean, he'd come in here moments before. I guess he was taking a pizza home to his dad or something. Now that's a sad situation," Deena said. "Probably about kill a parent to lose a kid, especially with his girl off wherever the hell she is and not checking in."

I nodded at that. Deena handed me the bread-sticks and I paid for them. I get a friends and family discount because I'm next door, so I didn't have to pay full price. The garlic smell got me, and I was munching on them on the way home.

I was turning down onto the long country road that would take me home when my cell phone rang. Byron's name showed up on my dash, which was where the Bluetooth fed into. I told the car to answer the phone.

"What's up?" I asked, setting down the bread-stick, like he could see me driving one handed with the food in my mouth.

"Are you busy this evening?" Byron asked. "I was thinking of coming by. I've kind of hit a wall on this death and only a couple of minor things have crossed my desk today. If you can, I thought we'd have dinner and then I'd get to work on the carriage house."

"Sounds good," I said. "I have no idea what Win is making, but I was just at Deena's and she gave me some breadsticks." Which was true enough, I guess, though she hadn't actually pressed them on me the way I made it sound. She'd just smartly made the suggestion when my stomach growled.

Byron agreed that that would work for him and said he'd be at the house in about forty-five minutes or so. Win would probably not have dinner for an hour, so he was timing it just about right. The weather was decent enough that he could get a good look at what needed to be done in the carriage house and plan for whatever work he wanted to do that evening. If I was unlucky, I'd be roped into helping out. While I don't enjoy doing construction work, I could always see what information I could get from Byron about the murder.

I started to turn down the driveway to the house, having hung up. I narrowly avoided hitting a car that appeared out of nowhere. I slammed on the breaks just in time, watching as it went speeding down the street in the opposite direction. My heart pounded and my hands were sweating.

I took a breath, making sure it was clear before starting my turn.

Glancing in the rearview mirror as I pulled into the drive, inputting my key code, waiting for the gates to open, I saw the car that had nearly hit me come screaming to a halt as if it was going to try and follow me into the driveway.

Chapter 13

The car turning into the drive behind me was actually a big old SUV, white, with windows that were tinted dark enough that I couldn't see through them. It rode higher than my Honda Fit, and I was thankful for the narrow car as I squeezed through the gates before they had finished opening. I quickly hit the button to close them again. If the SUV came through there would be damage to it.

The gates we had at the drive were mostly decorative black iron joining to stone columns on either side of the drive. You had to have the combination to get in or else call up to the house. Anyone with business normally came through the gates at the stables, which would be open during the day when most people came for business. For after hours, those gates also had a combination lock, that one much fancier. Boarders all got their own combination, which we removed when they stopped boarding with us. We had a general code for veterinarians and emergency workers who might need to get to the horses.

The gates were slowly closing as I drove carefully up the drive. It's mostly paved, turning to gravel only near the house, something I was going to change as soon as we finished the carriage house. I wanted cement all the way around so that when it rained I wasn't hopping over puddles. The SUV stayed where it was, grill pressing up close to the black gates as if it were trying to intimidate them.

I couldn't see anyone inside nor did I see a front license plate, not even a decorative one.

I considered getting out and going back to the gate to get a better look until I realized it was possible the driver had a weapon. I had no idea why someone would try to hit my car, not once, but twice.

It was possible this was a sort of road rage given that I had nearly hit them moments ago, but given what had happened to Duke Quint, I couldn't help but think that there was more going on.

By the time I got to the garage, I was shaking. I was nearly afraid to walk around to the house.

While the gate is high, the low stone fencing around the edge of the property wasn't going to stop an intruder. It was only about three to four feet high, depending upon the incline of the land. We had black split-rail fencing beyond, but people can easily climb over it. We didn't use barbed wire or anything.

I finally convinced myself that with everything that happened, someone would hear me start to scream if I saw someone who shouldn't be there. I got out of my car slowly, carrying my breadsticks, which I had almost forgotten. I wondered if I should leave them and come back with Morgan. Except, if there was someone and they were dangerous, both Morgan and I could be hurt.

I carried my stuff out of the garage, closing the door with the keypad behind me, and then hurried over to the house. We'd set up alarm systems that would go off if someone tried to open the garage door or really any door around the house. We also had cameras at the front gate. I'd be able to see if someone had climbed over the wall beyond the pillars.

Byron had recommended it after the carriage house had burned down. He'd been concerned because with Jaci working with drug dealers, some users might try and get onto the property. We'd had cameras around the house after I was attacked in the carriage house. We had always had cameras around the barn. Now we had cameras at all the gates. Pretty soon, we'd have cameras everywhere.

I smelled the faintest hint of freshly mown grass, probably the last of the year given how the weather was changing. I heard the normal sounds of the evening, a horse whinnying, the faintest of shush sounds as a slight breeze moved through the trees, a few branches scraping together, their leaves already starting to fall.

No sounds of anyone rushing towards me or trying to catch me before I made it to the house. I walked along, trying not to kick at the gravel lest it allow someone else to mask their steps.

My heart was beating too loudly for me to hear anything but the sound of blood rushing in my ears. I was no longer hungry, and if I had to, I'd drop that box of breadsticks in a hot minute to flee. Although later, when I was calm, I'd be pissed off at myself. Deena's breadsticks are wonderful. I'd say to die for, but clearly that wasn't the case.

Morgan opened the door as I fumbled about the lock with my keys. I had had the presence of mind to keep them out, but I was shaking too hard to get them into the lock. Fortunately, he's always listening. He likes the cameras because now he can just watch me come up the driveway when he hears the ping from the gate.

"Who was that in the white SUV?" he asked.

"I don't know, but they almost hit me as I was turning. Then they turned around and would have rear-ended me if I hadn't gotten through the gate. No one followed me through the gates or over the fence, did they?"

"Not that I saw, but I was mostly watching where you were," Morgan said.

I went into the kitchen and set down the breadsticks. Win gave them a look but to her credit, she didn't sniff. Still, she might have in another life. I gave her a wan smile. I'd have laughed in another situation.

"Byron will be here later," I said, though really it was probably down to about half an hour. He'd probably get there not long after Morgan and I finished finding the video footage I wanted to see. I'd be able to report any intruders then, if necessary.

The cameras fed to a system set up in the office. I used to think of it as Gram's office, all green and cream. There were light wood bookshelves behind a light wood desk, something far too sunny for the traditional study, but very serviceable. Gram had only had a small computer that she used there. I upgraded that as well as adding a monitor just for the security feeds. That had gone on the shelves behind the desk, the low ones that had the painting of a girl and her cats over it, breaking up the shelving.

Hellspark and Babs were in their favorite spot, the window seat near the desk. The vent from the heater blew down from there and I think that it blew hard enough that they could feel the warmth. In the summertime, the sun came through and both cats loved basking in it. Currently they were curled together into one large cat as only Siamese seem to be able to do.

I am not quite the Siamese cat snob that Gram was, but they were the cats I was most familiar with.

I settled in the chair behind the desk, turning around as Morgan went between the desk and the window seat to work the controls on the computer to run the recordings.

I had opted for color security, which was supposed to make it easier to see details. Unfortunately, the quality wasn't quite there, but it was good enough. If the SUV had had a front license plate, we could have read it. If the glass hadn't been tinted, we could have seen a face behind it. Unfortunately, the glass was just as tinted in the recording and there wasn't much to see. I made out the slight outline of a head as a darker shadow behind the tinted glass.

The SUV sat there for a few moments, no doubt watching me drive away. When they backed up and left, I hoped that it would turn at an angle to give us a view of the license plate, but the driver steered far enough back to turn around on the street rather than in the drive, even though the small portion of the drive before the gates was wide enough for people to turn around in. It wasn't the safest way to turn around, given how people drive country roads, but clearly safety was not their top priority.

Someone didn't want me to see the plates, anticipating the cameras. Too bad. But at least I made sure no one had come onto the property after me, at least not yet.

"Well, that's that," I said.

"I think you should call Byron," Morgan said.

"I'll tell him when he gets here. He's coming for dinner. We were going to work on the carriage house, after." I stood up from the computer. Hellspark gave me a glare, but Babs ignored me.

"Have you been poking around in that boy's death?" Morgan asked.

"That's what's so weird," I said. "Not really. I mean I've been listening to people talk, but I haven't been asking questions. Daisy talked to Mom and that's about it. That would probably be the closest thing to an interrogation. Cheri doesn't really ask questions, she just listens to gossip at the coffee shop."

Morgan nodded. "So why would someone want to hit your car?"

That I didn't know. I shook my head.

"I think maybe Byron needs to know in case someone is after you to scare him, don't you think?" Morgan suggested.

Morgan's suggestion sounded farfetched, but this was a person who had caused an accident injuring a bunch of other people just to murder one man. They didn't care about anyone but their target. I shivered and went to find my handbag where I'd left my phone.

Before I could pick up, I heard the sound of a car driving up beside the house. Looking out the back window, as the car had kept going, I noted it was Byron's truck. He'd already arrived.

I hurried to the door, opening it as he got there.

"I have some news," he said. His whole face was somber.

"What?"

"We're being pulled off the car accident, at least for now. Although no one really believes that it was an accident, there's nothing there to suggest where we go next. I just got the call a few minutes ago." Byron's voice was flat, the way it got when he was upset but didn't want to show it.

"I need to tell you something that might be related," I said. I gave him a brief rundown of the near miss I had had coming onto the property.

Byron shook his head. "You can't be sure it

has anything to do with Quint. You haven't been asking questions, have you?"

"Keeping my ear to the ground but mostly just listening," I said. "Any questions would be ordinary. Half of Seales probably knows as much as I know, and some of the other half probably know more."

Byron nodded. "So it can't be related. It has to be something else."

"Unless they want to scare you into backing down," I said, offering Morgan's suggestion.

Bryon stood there giving me a long look. "Do you really think things like that work?"

I shook my head.

"You might want to add more security. This might be someone still angry about Jaci. They could want to get back at the farm. You *were* involved in that. Even if this does have to do with me and this investigation, extra security is a good idea."

Byron took off walking down the long driveway. It's over a quarter of a mile and I hurried to keep up, feeling the chill breeze ripping at my shirt. I'd left my jacket in the house, in the study, though Morgan had no doubt taken it to a closet to hang it up.

Still, there was no way I was going to miss out on what was going on if Byron was investigating.

When we got to the gate, I was surprised to

see it open. I glanced at Byron to see if he'd left it open.

He was shaking his head, looking around. Clearly, he thought he'd closed it when he entered. Which meant there was a possibility that someone else was on the property.

Chapter 14

I wrapped my arms around my body. Even without the wind, the night was cool. When the breeze came up, just a gentle one lightly tugging at my clothing, I shivered. I really needed a jacket or a sweater or something to help me keep warm. I smelled the grass and the faintest hint of horse blown towards me on the breeze.

Byron stood there, studying the gate, the light still bright enough for me to see the frown on his face as he did so.

"I take it you closed it again when you came through?" I asked. Byron had the key code so he could come and go as he liked. I couldn't imagine that he hadn't closed it. He was the one always talking to me about safety and making sure things were locked and closed up.

"I did," Byron said, walking around, looking at the ground. I didn't follow him. I knew he was looking for tracks. The cement drive was mostly clear, a bit of mud, but there's nearly always some mud between me, Daisy, Win, and Morgan, not to mention visitors who come and go, most calling the house so Morgan can open the gate for them. The mud wasn't a sign that someone else was there.

"We should go back and look at the video. See who opened it. And how." I said.

Byron glanced at me. "You go. I'm calling this in. I don't like that someone tried to hit your car and then we find the gate open."

I hurried up the lane. I knew Byron was watching. There were plenty of trees around so if someone had gotten in, they plenty of places to hide. They could be watching for a chance to attack. I hoped that I had time to scream before they did.

I was running before I knew it, thankful that I wear black athletic shoes to work. They were comfortable and looked fine with my slacks. Now and then I wore Mary Janes with a skirt, but always flats. If I had to, I could usually run.

That wasn't the reason for my fashion choices, or lack thereof. I needed to be able to move around the treatment table. I also like to be comfortable. If that meant I could run in whatever shoes I wore, so much the better, considering how often my life had been in danger since I returned home.

I made it to the house. Morgan poked his head out almost immediately.

"What's wrong?" he asked.

"The gate's open and Byron remembers closing it," I said, panting slightly. I'm not in good running shape apparently. I ought to do it more often, but then closed that thought off. I'm not big on running.

"Do I need to call the police?" Morgan asked.

"No. But we do want to watch the security footage from the time Byron came through until now," I said. "He's calling this in. He doesn't like that someone almost hit me and now the gate's open."

Morgan nodded and followed me to the office. I could have done it myself, but I knew that he liked to be sure he was on top of any sort of problem. I heard Daisy talking to Win in the kitchen. I wondered if I should warn them. I could do that as soon as I looked at the footage to see who had come in or if the gate was left open just to scare us.

"How exactly would someone do that?" Morgan asked, pacing near the entry while I pulled up the footage. "They'd need a code."

"Unless Byron didn't wait until the gate was

completely closed and they stopped it, somehow?" I couldn't imagine Byron not waiting to be sure the thing was closed, though.

I went back to about the time I figured Byron would have entered the drive. Nothing for a few minutes while I did a slow fast forward. I slowed it to normal speed when his car came into view.

I watched Byron's hand reach out to the keypad on the narrow post between the gates. You have to look for the keypad. Gram had been advised to work on keeping it as unobtrusive as possible. Before I got used to it, half the time I had to get out of the car to reach it. I noticed it appeared that Byron had to stretch.

Byron's car drove in through the gates and then they started closing. I saw the lights from the back of his car—he was too far in for me to see the car itself—waiting, the red shining on the gates. Then the gate was closed and the red light from the brakes disappeared.

I kept watching. Soon enough, someone walked up to the gate, dressed in dark clothing and a hoodie with the hood up, obscuring their face. A dark pack rested on their back.

They did something to the keypad. Then they stood back, waiting. Finally, they felt around in the backpack and pulled out an item I couldn't make out. They worked on the keypad for a minute. The gates slowly opened.

When that happened, they hurried onto the property.

I looked up to see Morgan standing there, glowering.

"What did you notice?" I asked.

"The first time. They put in a code, expecting it to work, but it didn't. We changed the codes after you were cleared in Marty's death," Morgan said. "So whoever came in may have known her or came here when she was still alive but not since you were cleared."

I nodded. "Either that or they knew someone who did."

Morgan shrugged. "They knew where the box was and they knew how to use it."

"Lots of farms have security like ours," I said.

Morgan shrugged.

I called Byron to let him know about the video. Then I went out to the main room.

"What's going on?" Daisy called from the kitchen. "Dinner's almost ready."

"I doubt we'll be there," I said. "I barely missed being hit coming home and then someone left the gate open. Morgan and I saw someone enter the property after Byron drove in."

I heard a chair push away as Daisy hurried over to where I stood in the little mudroom area.

"Be careful," she said. "I was reading up on some things about the old car dealer on the corner. You know how we talked about why someone would want Duke to die there? Did you know his father once worked at that dealer? Just for a short time before he got something a little better."

"You think it ties into that?"

Daisy shrugged. "I don't know how, but it might. It just means that you really need to be careful."

"Except I haven't been asking questions. I mean, I'm just listening to what everyone said. I found that piece of paper and that's it. Byron couldn't even use it as evidence because I could have found the paper anywhere," I said. "At least when someone was after me for Marty, I understood that. And with Layla, she was outside my office, but I haven't done anything to warrant this!"

Daisy came over and enveloped me in one of her mom hugs. It was one of the things I liked about her. My mom hugs, but not like Aunt Daisy. My mom worries about what people think far too much.

When she was done Daisy took hold of my chin, as if I were five instead of closer to thirty-five, and looked at me. "I know that. But does everyone know that? I mean you have a reputation. And you were at the accident. You talked to people as you helped them. There may be something you didn't find that they think is important."

That niggling sense at the base of my skull, where I always felt things when I needed to pay attention, said that felt right. Penelope Blue didn't immediately appear, so while it might be important to remember, it wasn't a key thing. Penelope Blue had a tendency to appear only when something was really important.

She'd shown up on my bed the day I found the office where I was. She'd started pawing at me like she wanted to play. In fact, she even had a little mouse with feathers, one of her favorite toys when she'd been alive, and jumped around on the bed. It turned out the office was affordable and the location was good, even if it wasn't what I had had in mind. I just hadn't been able to find anything downtown.

"Someone else might have found something and they don't know what they have," I said.

"That could be," Daisy said, "but there's no way to know who or what might have been found. I think what we need to concentrate on is the fact that apparently you've been targeted. Someone thinks you found something or saw something while you were there. Has anything happened to Deanna or Dr. Sparks or anyone like that?"

Dr. Sparks was the chiropractor who worked a couple of doors down in my building.

I shook my head. "I was just in talking to Deanna, too," I said.

"I know," Daisy smiled.

At first I thought her mysterious smile was about the fact that she was psychic, too, but then I remembered the breadsticks. Of course. I'd only have gotten a bunch on a whim if I was in the pizza place, probably chatting with the owner.

"She asked if I had gotten caught in the traffic down there the other day, and then we talked about people stopping in for pizza, or not. She got some business but not as much as she had hoped. I think I saw her up in the parking lot looking down at the accident with a bunch of other people that night."

Daisy nodded. "But she might have noticed something you couldn't, at least about the people involved."

"I should call her and let her know about someone breaking in," I said.

I tried the pizza place but was told that Deanna was too busy to come to the phone. Looking at the time, they were probably swamped. Deanna does a lot of the heavy lifting and baking, and she's the first to say no calls during busy times. They let me leave a message, but I had no idea if Deanna would actually call me back. She'd probably do it for a customer, but she might or might not for something that was likely personal. If I had a problem with the breadsticks, I'd tell her next time I came in.

That left us with nothing to do but wait for Byron. I watched out the front dining room window. We never use the dining room, but it has a window that faces the front yard. I stood there, in the dark, accompanied by the large table and the heavy sideboard that came from another era. The china cabinet hovered along the other wall, the old, fine china still inside behind beveled glass. The glass was supposed to keep dust down, but I knew that even so, whether it would be used or not, Morgan and Win would take it out and wash it every few months.

Red and blue flashing lights signaled that the police had arrived to help Byron. I saw dark figures wandering around the yard, flashlights held to the ground, though it wasn't yet full dark, just a bit of dusk. I had a feeling they were looking to see if they could find traces of the intruder and perhaps track him or her to where they were hiding.

The doors were all locked on the house. Morgan had already set the alarm. Too much had happened over the last year or so that now we took precautions. Gram would no doubt have had a fit. She was of the era when you just left doors unlocked and let friends and relatives come in as they wanted, though in her case, Morgan or the man who had preceded him would do the door opening before anyone could just walk in.

I watched silently until my phone buzzed with a text.

Byron. Telling me they'd caught someone. I grabbed a jacket and went back out to see who might have been wandering around our property.

Chapter 15

The sun was going down fast as I hurried out of the house to get to Byron. Outside, the day smelled of old pine. The wind had had picked up a bit more. Though the sky was still clear, it felt like a storm was coming

I was glad of my jacket. I hurried down the drive, keeping to the center and making sure there weren't any places marked that I shouldn't walk. I didn't want to mess anything up, or worse, walk into a trap that might have been set by the intruder.

My imagination ran wild. I thought about guns being set up on a trip wire, waiting for me to pass. I thought of trees cut to fall down just as I passed under them. All of these things were more likely in a movie than in real life, but that didn't stop my heart from beating faster than it should. It also kept me walking as fast as possible until I got within the circle of red and blue lights where the police stood talking. A shadow was in the back of a car that Byron was leaning over.

I slowed down, listening, but the officers were all talking too softly for me to hear. One squad car drove off while the other, the one with the shadow in back, perhaps my intruder, waited with Byron. The driver of that car was talking to Byron. He was too far away for me to say for certain, but I thought that from his size and shape it might be Officer Springer.

Springer wasn't my favorite of the police officers—of course, that was silly to compare considering I was dating Byron, who would be by default my favorite, wouldn't he? However, Springer had intimated that he didn't trust Morgan simply because of the color of his skin. I hadn't liked the way he treated Morgan, which meant I didn't much like him. However, Springer had been nothing but nice to me, which was more than I could say for several of the other officers.

I always had a hard time figuring out who worked for the city and who was a sheriff as the police department here wasn't that big, but big enough that I didn't know everyone. Bryon was pretty much the only detective, getting the more serious cases that needed a full investigation.

While it might sound surprising to anyone listening to me talk about the murders that had happened around me, murders didn't happen in Seales that often.

"Who was it?" I asked when I got close enough to Byron that he could hear me without me screaming. I was suddenly uncertain if I'd be allowed closer to the car given that it was actual police property and I wasn't an officer, just a homeowner.

"You know a Craig Roland?" Byron asked.

I shook my head. "I don't. Does he know me?"

"He won't say." Byron turned back. "He said he was told come here, which he did. He was also told how to jump the fence. He says he drives a gray Hyundai sedan which is parked over by the entrance to the barn. Officers found one meeting its description by the side of the road. We're checking."

"So he wasn't in the car that tried to hit me." I wrapped my arms around myself again, thinking.

"Could have borrowed a car, but I don't see why," Byron said.

I kept coming back to the name. It sounded familiar, but I couldn't put my finger on it. I searched back over the last few days. Had Thad mentioned a Craig? I didn't think so. Thad was dating Lucas and used to be in love with Sean, both of whom came up in the course of the conversation and peripheral to the investigation.

I loved Thad to death. He's not always trusting because people have betrayed him simply based on his sexual preferences. I can't say I blame him for that lack of trust. However, I don't think he'd try and do something to hurt me or be involved in anyway.

If Thad knew about a Craig, I had a feeling he'd have mentioned it. I'd have remembered the name, too, at least I hoped I would. Even if I would otherwise forget, if Craig's name had been mentioned and it was important, Penelope Blue would have made an appearance and made me notice her the moment Thad talked about him.

Byron tapped the top of the car and looked at Officer Springer. Springer got in and made a K-turn to head back out to the road with his passenger inside.

Byron sighed.

"No dinner?" I said.

"I think I can make dinner. Maybe sitting around in the interview room for a few will make him more talkative," Byron said. "But I think we're off about working on the carriage house."

That was too bad. The way things were going, it was never going to be finished. At least that's how it felt.

Maybe next year it would be. Maybe by next

year I'd feel safe enough to move back out there. Or maybe Byron and I would be serious enough that he'd just move in with me. Things were going that way, but it still felt early, particularly since I didn't have my own place and didn't stay at his very often.

"I'm sure Win will have things ready for us and you can get some food in you before heading off to work." I leaned against him as we walked up the drive.

"It seems like every time we get into a bit of a routine, a big case comes up and things get all jumbled again," Byron said. "Here I had this idea that living in a small town would mean slightly more regular hours."

"Silly you," I said. And silly me probably, too. After all, I wanted a more regular relationship where I could count on him. Unfortunately, I knew that was unlikely to happen if I were dating a police officer.

Morgan got the door as we came inside.

I was ready for a pleasant dinner, planning my evening after Byron left seeing we wouldn't be working out on the carriage house. Little did I know I'd be seeing him again before the evening was over.

Chapter 16

Daisy and Byron and I chatted through dinner. As usual, it was in the nook next to the kitchen. In summer, when the sun is still out at dinner time, you can see the lawn with the plants around the edges. You could even see the side of the carriage house which had once been lined with flowering shrubs. The crepe myrtle that was the sort of showpiece of the lawn was perfectly placed to be seen by those sitting in the kitchen area.

Gram had had good eye for what caught the eye and created a pleasant atmosphere.

In winter, the nook was cozy. Win had pulled the blinds, which were fabric blinds in earth tones designed to blend into the Tuscan decorated kitchen. It was looking dated. The craze had been getting popular the last time Gram had updated. I had no plans to change it because everything in the kitchen worked well and flowed with colors that were woven through the rest of the house.

Abby, my sister-in-law who lives in Charlotte, was dying to redo the kitchen into something more modern. She was thinking black and white and gray. That all sounded rather cool and dull. Daisy and I liked the warmth of the browns even if the Tuscan look was a bit overdone and a bit out of fashion.

The table we sat around was small and seated up to four people. It was a pine wood and the chairs were square and comfortable. Daisy often worked at her computer there between meals. Because Byron was joining us, Win had fancied the table up with placemats that had an autumn leaf pattern on them.

While I brought breadsticks, Win had made a roast chicken. The smells were heavenly, and I was sorry that she hadn't made her biscuits, though the breadsticks had been re-warmed nicely and added a bit of zing to the meal.

At the last minute, realizing someone else would be there, Win had even whipped up a blueberry crumble. While the berries weren't fresh, it being too late in the season for that, the frozen ones she'd found were very tasty. As always, her crumble smelled heavenly and tasted even better.

As we filled up, talking about food and general gossip, time passed quickly. Byron realized he had to leave as he finished his last bite of crumble, feeling a bit embarrassed that he'd left Craig Roland to cool his heels for quite as long as he had.

After Byron left, I spent time with Aunt Daisy. We go through phases of spending time together and then being on our own. I rather like it. This time we were discussing Halloween and if we wanted to do something about the house. It's not like we're on a street where kids will come.

"I'd love to have some sort of party here where everyone dressed up," Daisy said. "I love Halloween."

I did too. We started brainstorming ideas about whether to have an open house where we gave out candy to kids. I could promote it to patients and if it was a general open house, we could get Cheri to promote it at the coffee shop. It would be easy enough to use Facebook to get the word out, too. Seales had a community group for things like that, too.

Or we could just have a smaller party for friends.

"I'm feeling as if I want to open the place up to the larger world," Daisy said. "I'd like to get a sense of how the house feels with strangers in it. Your Gram never really did that much. It was always family, except of course for that one holiday party. If I'm going to think about a business that opens up the property, whether it's a B&B or maybe just a place for events, I want to get a sense of the flow, so this would be perfect."

It gave me a tingle to think that Daisy was taking the B&B idea so seriously. If she did do it, I had no doubt it would end up working out fabulously for her and, by extension, me. It wouldn't happen right away. We'd be spending time planning and working on things, which would give Byron time to finish up my little carriage house. As we talked, I couldn't help but notice Penelope Blue was oddly absent. Perhaps this wasn't such a good idea after all. Or maybe it just wasn't that important.

In fact, the little ghost cat didn't appear until I got a phone call much later that night, after I retired to the bedroom. Byron.

I'd been forced to get up and walk across the room as I don't keep the phone next to the bed. I might not be completely paranoid about the whole Wi-Fi thing, but I liked to be at least a little cautious. Across the room was good enough for me. The covers were tossed open beautifully, and my sheets were cream in the dim light from my phone when I picked it up.

"What's up?" I asked, trying to keep a yawn out of my voice.

"There's been an accident," Byron said. "There's a woman who works at the pizza place by your clinic that was just hit by another car pretty hard—hard enough to flip her car around and send it into the far lane. She's unconscious and in the hospital, but alive. I'm worried this is connected to the accident the other day. Someone might think there was something for people to see from the vantage of your business and we don't know what it is."

"It wasn't Deena, was it?" I asked.

"You know her well?" Byron replied.

"We talk. We're not like good friends who hang out, but we work next door to each other, so we talk. She always gives me a discount. It's where I got the breadsticks. In fact, she motioned me into the place this evening to chat about the accident. Mostly she complained that she didn't get as much business as she thought she might considering how backed up traffic was. She also told me Duke worked for her a long time ago when she had her business downtown. She said he seemed nice enough but that her till was always short when he worked there, and that ended when he left."

"That's interesting," Byron said. "I hadn't heard that about him."

"It's a small thing," I said. "The gossip I hear is that he seemed like a nice guy but was smarmy when you got close to him. Things happened, but he never got blamed even though pretty much everyone was certain he had a hand in something, you know?"

Byron was making a note. "I called to warn you that the car trying to hit you might have been after you because of something they think you saw. You were down on the street, so you might not have seen it, or maybe you did. Be safe. A car will patrol your street a bit more regularly than normal, just in case. I mean we caught a guy, but he hasn't said much."

"Did this guy say why he was at the house or anything about who asked him to do it?"

"Clammed up, asked for a lawyer and said nothing. He's going to get charged with trespassing but that's about it. The fine for trespassing isn't enough to make him talk more than he already is."

Which was too bad.

"Unfortunately, because no one was hurt and we can't prove that he vandalized anything, that's all we have him on. Trespassing isn't a felony."

"I wish there were a way to make him say something. I swear I've heard his name somewhere, but I don't remember where," I said. "I know it was in connection with Duke Quint, but I can't quite recall how or where."

"I'll make a note of that, too," Byron said. "I

asked if he knew Quint, and he admitted to it and that he didn't like him. Didn't say anything about wanting him dead but wasn't happy with him at all."

"Thanks for calling to let me know about Deena. I'll have to go visit her tomorrow afternoon," I said.

"Call first. I don't know how long the hospital will keep her for. The accident was plenty bad, but she was really lucky."

I said I would and started to climb back into bed, but then I started thinking about Duke's death. I stretched for a moment and got on the computer. I'd regret it in the morning, but there were a few things I wanted to check.

I looked up Duke's Facebook page and looked through the condolences. I found Craig Roland's comment and I realized that was why the name stuck with me. He was glad Duke was dead and not afraid to say something.

Penelope Blue showed up and started prancing around on the desk for a few seconds and then settled off to the side while she washed a ghost paw, keeping an eye on me as I worked. Clearly this was something important.

I searched through Craig Roland's timeline but didn't see anything immediately interesting. He had things pretty locked down, so I couldn't see much, but there was a girlfriend who tagged him frequently and her Facebook page was much more public.

I checked through her timeline. There wasn't much interesting until I noticed she and I had a mutual friend. Thad. I checked on timeline and started cross-checking the mutual friends Thad had with Craig's girlfriend, a woman by the name of Stephanie.

There was Lucas, Sean, and even Craig was a mutual friend. Those who hadn't locked down their friends list, like Craig, also listed Duke Quint as a friend. I frowned and wondered what was up and what Thad might have told me if I had known to ask. Who was Craig Roland and Stephanie Leads, and what did Thad know about them? Why was Craig at my house in the middle of the night?

I considered calling Thad right then, but Thad would either be with Lucas or he'd be asleep. If I interrupted him or woke him up, I'd be less likely to get the information I wanted. Better to catch him tomorrow, perhaps around lunch time, and drop my intruder information on him. Maybe he'd be able to tell me something then.

I was reminded what Daisy said about the used car place, so I started doing a search on that, too. Nothing much there, really. I was going to have to check in with the newspaper to see if there were articles in the morgue. There certainly wasn't anything online.

Tomorrow was Saturday. Fortunately I only had two patients in the morning. I was working towards having Saturday off. Right now I was just working on getting a full schedule. After that I'd figure out what hours I liked best and worked for the majority of my patients. Then I'd find time to do paperwork around those hours. Of course, maybe I ought to work in time to do midweek sleuthing.

Not that I'm a detective or anything. And wouldn't it better if we just had no more murders? I sighed and shut off the computer. Penelope Blue was still there on the desk, but she'd settled into a little ball and was snoozing away. When I turned off my computer, she faded out like she was part of the screen's background.

I smiled at the image and then climbed into bed where I had trouble falling asleep. I was too worked up with questions now, knowing that Deena had been hurt. It was silly, really, to hit someone driving with a car. Deena was just fine. She wasn't dead.

Someone had just made the fact that Duke had been murdered even more obvious. If they hadn't tried to hurt me and then succeeded in hurting Deena, no one would have connected the accident to anything else. Unless, like Craig's trespassing, this was all just something to muddy the waters to keep us looking for something that didn't exist.

It hit me then that perhaps we were completely missing something. Not just about why Duke was murdered but perhaps something that his murder was designed to cover up. Penelope Blue appeared on the bed near my pillow and her little body seemed to shake and move as the little ghost cat started to purr.

Chapter 17

The next day, a patrol car followed me to work and then home again. It felt weird, like I was doing something wrong. It was also frustrating because I felt I had to drive perfectly. I might have a bit of a lead foot otherwise. It also made me feel as if I were under suspicion again.

I had flashbacks of Claire Wilcox following me and how she'd been murdered outside my parent's house when I was living there. The last thing I needed was a repeat of that episode of my life.

By the time Sunday rolled around, I was ready to let someone else do the driving and let them be followed by a cop.

I woke around eight, which is late for me. I smelled cinnamon and sugar and knew Win was baking again. I heard movement upstairs, which meant Daisy hadn't gone down yet, either. I got up and dressed quickly in jeans and a sweater.

I checked my phone to be sure I wasn't overdressed, but the weather app assured me that if anything I was underdressed. We were going into one of those polar vortex things which was bringing unseasonably cold air. We were due for our first frost. Halloween wasn't even until next week.

Gram had always had Morgan decorate for Halloween early. Daisy and I hadn't, but now that we were planning the party, having decided to advertise the open house, we needed to get something done.

Win had already been shopping, going to several different places for a variety of candies and non-candy treats. She was a good shopper and had probably raided every variety of dollar store within ten miles. She'd also found some new decorations as well as the ones tucked away in the attic. I was starting to get into the mood of having visitors.

When I got downstairs, I saw that Morgan and Win had already pulled out most of the boxes from the attic. Gram had always wanted a basement for storage, but the house didn't have one. There had been a sort of cellar that had once been accessible from outside—it had long since been cemented over—and now we just had a larger than normal crawl space but not a full basement. Once a year we had people check the screens around the edges to be sure nothing was open and a raccoon or, worse, a stray cat, couldn't get down there and be trapped.

So, the attic was the area where everything got stored and forgotten about. At some point, I ought to go up there and sort through things. That wasn't a job I was looking forward to. It didn't seem very pressing, either.

Morgan pulled down things now and then. Once down, I'd sort a box here and there with his help. I hadn't actually gone up to look around there myself. It had been hard going through Gram's things in her bedroom, which was why I hadn't changed anything in there. I had no desire to go through generations of stuff that might be hidden up there. I'd have Daisy help, of course, and I'd probably need my mom there as well so I'd know who some of the stuff had belonged to. That was a task for another time.

The forecast for Halloween was actually pretty good. It was supposed to be clear and cool but not cold. Last year it had poured rain, and, in many cities, they'd held trick or treating the day before. On the actual night of Halloween, trees had blown down and there were flash floods all over. Fortunately, we were not getting a repeat of that.

Breakfast was French toast, which was why I'd been smelling cinnamon and sugar.

"This looks great," I said to Win. I always wondered how she knew when to prepare food to have it ready for us.

She smiled and nodded at me. Daisy came down about then, oohing when she saw what was for breakfast.

"Are we ready to decorate?" I asked.

"I will be," Daisy said. "Have you heard anything more about Deena's accident or Duke Quint's death?"

"Deena got out of the hospital yesterday and she's been home, sore and pissed. She didn't really see who hit her. It was dark. Word was, it was a white SUV, but that doesn't mean anything because there are tons of those."

"But the SUV that almost hit you was white, which means that it could be the same person."

"I just don't know why. It only makes it seem like they have something to hide. I keep thinking it's a misdirection, but what aren't we supposed to be looking at that we might be?"

Daisy sighed. "We're looking at Duke. Maybe that's all they want us to avoid because it's obvious if we investigate him."

"Byron has been," I said. "There's no wife.

Duke's ex moved to Columbus about two months ago. It's one reason they broke up. Distance. Byron said she said nothing bad about him."

"If she were guilty, she'd be foolish to do so," Daisy pointed out.

I smiled.

"I doubt his father had anything to do with it. I looked at the used car place but didn't find much out. I told Byron about it though, in case that was a clue. The owner sold and moved to Florida. Nothing really about him online. I guess he died a few years after moving down there," I continued, taking a bite of the French toast.

Someone had turned on some music to decorate by and there was some fancy fiddling going on, an old song about the Devil and Johnny dueling it out.

Daisy was nodding her head along to the beat, thinking.

"I remember Bud working there vaguely," she said. "Did Byron ask him why he quit?"

"Got a better job. It's been so long that other than general information, we can't really get confirmation about why."

"The place was a dump, but I know a lot of kids got their first cars there. Usually regretted it, but kids then just felt lucky to get a car at all, even if it didn't run half the time."

"Dad and I looked there but he didn't like anything I liked." I smiled at the memory.

"I wanted to look through old newspapers," I added. "I started at the library, but their papers didn't go back that far. They sent me to the newspaper office, but it was closed. It seems like they're always closed unless you make an appointment."

"You ought to."

"I don't want Byron to think I'm investigating. I don't really want anyone to think I'm investigating, not after what's happened."

"But we need to know what happened on that corner. Besides the car dealer. I mean I suppose it could be that Bud sold someone a car and their child died. They wouldn't even have to live in Seales, so we might not have heard much."

"Maybe they didn't die," I said. "Maybe they were just hurt."

"But they wanted Duke dead," Daisy said.

"Did they? Or did they just want him injured?"

We cleaned our plates and I continued to think about the case. After rinsing them and putting them in the dishwasher for later—Win was out in the yard with Morgan getting decorations out of their boxes—I went upstairs, still thinking.

I had tried to call Thad a couple of times, but

he hadn't answered my calls. I got my phone and tried again.

Once again, it rang through to voicemail. This time I left a message telling him that it was okay if he didn't want to talk to me, but please let me know that he was okay. I was starting to get a bad feeling about things.

Chapter 18

The morning was cold, and I had to wear a heavier coat than I expected to help decorate. Despite the chill, the day smelled pleasantly of damp grass and that certain something that makes fall smell different from summer. It was going to be a clear day without a cloud in the sky. My nose turned red. A slight breeze rustled branches and you could hear the radio from inside as we decorated around the outside of the house.

The main front door got a Halloween wreath. We had strings of pumpkin lights to line the main windows of the house. Inside, Win put up one of those sheets that made it look like someone was trying to get out. It even had drops of blood, something that made me shiver.

Just inside the door we placed one of the big

motion-activated skeletons. It stood just about eye to eye with me and would be plenty creepy with a bit of Halloween music. Morgan had a large plastic caldron that he put near the door to the living room and started filling it with candy.

The dining room was cleaned so that we could use that space for bringing items out. When Gram and Grandpa had redesigned the house with the family in mind, they hadn't expected to host large parties for strangers. They figured anyone coming in would go through the house, so there was no easy entry access to the dining room, which made it rather useless for an open house.

"If I make it a bed and breakfast, it would work because only guests would eat there. We could even put in French doors," Daisy said, still thinking about the B&B. These things were always to be considered. If we just opened the land up for parties, we wouldn't need to worry about the oddly placed dining room.

When the paper skeletons and black cats and spiders were placed on windows and the plastic cat skeletons were placed in strategic places around the house, we called it good. Win had gotten paper streamers to make it even more festive, but we'd put those up later.

Our decorating only took a few hours. Byron arrived in time to help with the last of it. He got a glass of water before going out to work on the carriage house. I followed him.

"How are things going with Duke's murder?"

"Nothing is going," Byron said. "We haven't found a good reason someone might have almost hit you. We haven't found a reason for someone hitting Deena. Craig Roland isn't talking about anything at all, which surprises me. I'm wondering if he doesn't actually know anything because he seems like the kind of guy who'd crack under pressure."

"Maybe he just knows enough?" I suggested. "You know, that this had to do with Duke and that he needed to be on my property but not why. It's easier to keep a small secret than a big one."

"He's not even given me a name, which I thought he might."

"More scared of them than of you?"

Byron nodded. We were in the space where the kitchen would be. It had been plumbed professionally and the electrical was in, but the cabinets were missing. They were sitting in the big living area. Once again, it was going to be an open floor plan. Instead of having a bedroom hiding under the loft, I was going to have a big open office alcove back there. There'd be a bathroom downstairs, too. We'd debated a powder room versus a full bathroom and decided on a bath with a shower. That way if I ever redid the en suite, I could use that one until it was finished.

Upstairs was just a big loft with a private bath and a closet. It looked over the living area and made the whole space seem huge.

"I have to wonder what scares him," Byron said. "I know that Duke was killed, but it's like someone wants us to know that."

I sighed. "They killed other people too, like Kelly Ellis."

Penelope Blue showed up and wandered around the carriage house. She picked her feet up daintily as if she didn't want them to touch the raw subfloor and glared at me.

"Is it possible this is about Kelly Ellis, and with all our focus on Duke Quint, we're not paying attention to who would want to murder Ellis?" I asked.

Byron sighed. "The car made sure Duke's truck went off the road."

"Could that have been meant as a distraction? Maybe he was just in the wrong place at the wrong time?" Kelly Ellis was important to this.

"Duke's truck was messed up," Byron said. "That's why we're investigating."

"Maybe it was Duke's idea to murder Ellis and someone got him?" I said.

"Too convoluted," Byron said. "Crime is

simple unless you're watching a television show and they need strange motives."

"But we're not getting anywhere looking at Duke." I was squatting on the floor watching Byron remeasure where the cabinets would go so that we'd get everything straight before moving them in and placing them. Penelope Blue came up and practically leaped on my knees to get my attention.

I nodded at her, smiling a little. Byron was busy with the measure, so he didn't notice my interaction with the ghost cat. It probably would have looked strange to him if he had.

"Sometimes you just don't," Byron said. "I know that this is frustrating because for some reason someone thinks that you might have seen something. We've been talking to everyone who works up on your hill in case someone saw something, but nothing stands out."

I sighed, frustrated. If there was something to the idea that Kelly Ellis was the person targeted, I was going to have to find it. I knew that he and Duke knew each other because Ellis worked at the school. Duke would have had him for social studies just like I did.

Given what my mom had said, Ellis hadn't liked Duke any better than a lot of teachers. Supposedly Ellis's wife didn't want to move so far from their kids and that was what had kept him from

Florida. If Atlanta had been affordable, she'd have had them move there.

I chewed on that wondering why Ellis and his wife were suddenly talking about Atlanta. It had sounded like her staying there was planned and they'd be gone for some time. Cheri had even heard the occasional rumor that Mrs. Ellis had been house hunting. So what had changed that they could suddenly afford a house in Atlanta?

Had Ellis somehow just come into money? I felt the slightest tickle at the back of neck telling me that I was on the right track. Penelope Blue gave a final satisfied lick to her paw before fading out.

Chapter 19

After finishing up some work in the carriage house that included hammers and nails and lots of dust, Byron headed home for a shower. I headed into the Big House for my own shower. I had noticed Daisy going out to ride earlier. I hadn't noticed her come back, so I hoped I was beating her to it. I didn't want to run out of hot water.

That was another thing we were going to need to consider if she did the B&B. Hot water. Right now the hot water heater was barely enough for all of us living in the house. It'd be fine once I moved out. Morgan and Win had their own timing given that they ran the house. Daisy and I had ours. Sometimes we tripped each other up. A hot bath on an off time could leave someone else with a lukewarm shower that quickly turned chilly.

I made a mental note to talk to Daisy about hot water. A contractor or a planner would likely point out necessities such as that, however, it was a cost I'd have to add to the bottom line. I wasn't that worried about it. With the assets I had thanks to Gram, I could easily get a loan. But it meant that I wanted to be sure a B&B was the best thing we could do. Renting land for events would definitely be the easier of the two plans.

In fact, if we were serious about the B&B, I ought to invite my brother Bobbie and his wife to spend time in the house, staying there as guests. Daisy and I could get used to sharing our space with new people. My folks could even come by to create something of a crowd.

As I pondered the future, I wondered about the carriage house. It was basically one bedroom. Great for me now, but what if I wanted to have kids some day? Byron seemed to want to be a father and I'd always sort of saw myself as having a baby. I wasn't so young that I could consider putting that off forever, either. A baby would mean moving back into the big house unless I wanted to either build yet another house on the property or perhaps move off the property altogether.

Maybe the B&B wouldn't be such a good idea.

I turned on the hot water for the shower. It warmed up quickly. I finished and feeling cleaner than I had since I woke up, I called Cheri.

"What's up?" she asked. I heard the television in the background on low, but it was talk which meant it wasn't the radio. The voices were too distant for her to have people over. Besides, if she had someone other than Travis over, I'd have heard about it even if I wasn't invited.

"Just had a thought about the accident again. Have you got time to chat?"

"I wouldn't have picked up if I didn't. Travis is with his mom. She had a fall and they've gone to the hospital in Lexington. He called to tell me when he was already there so it wasn't like I could volunteer to hold his hand in the waiting room or anything." There was the slightest bit of pique in her voice. Cheri likes to be helpful.

"I hope she'll be okay," I said.

"It sounds like things are going well. They're worried about her ankle, so it's not like she's hurt her hip or anything, which I hear is really bad, so that's all good. I hope it's not a break though because doesn't it take older people longer to heal?"

We talked about Travis's mom for a bit and then got back to the matter at hand.

"So tell me more about your thoughts on the case. Does this mean Byron isn't taking you seriously again because otherwise I expect you'd have told him and he'd be investigating and you wouldn't be bouncing ideas off of me."

"Exactly," I said, laughing at Cheri's ability to sum things up in a hundred words or more. I told her my idea about Duke wanting to kill Mr. Ellis and maybe someone deciding he'd gone too far with killing and trying to hurt him.

"Ohh…" Cheri said. "That sounds like a movie or something."

If it was, I hadn't seen it.

"What I wanted to know was why Ellis and his wife were going to Atlanta to visit the kids now. Did you say something about them looking to move there?"

"I did," Cheri said decisively. "I know they'd decided against it early on because it's so expensive, but they were looking around at condos or something this time, maybe finding something a bit more in their price range, you know?"

"Condos aren't always that much cheaper," I said.

"I've never priced one." Cheri laughed. "I work in a coffee shop. Real estate is not my forte—although maybe it should be. I bet I'd be good at that. I'm a good listener. I just don't have it in me to work all on commission even if those commissions are pretty nice."

"I was wondering where Ellis got the money to spend on a condo in Atlanta when everyone knew they couldn't afford a house earlier. A condo really isn't that much cheaper unless they were going for something really tiny. It's possible," I said, but it didn't feel right. Penelope Blue wouldn't have been pointing me towards Ellis this time if I didn't need to follow up on that side of things.

"It also doesn't work because a car cut Duke off and he swerved. I suppose that means he caused the accident, but another car cut him off," Cheri said.

"What if they were supposed to be working together?" I asked. "You know, Duke and whoever cut him off."

Cheri and I chewed on that for a bit. I had a sense that Ellis was part of this and we needed to look at him because we'd been so focused on Duke. Someone wanted us to stay focused on Duke, even creating problems for those who might have witnessed something.

"I'll see what I can dig up about Duke and Mr. Ellis. Did your mom know anything?"

"Just that Mr. Ellis didn't like Duke any more than anyone else did," I said. "At least at the school. A few teachers loved him, but most didn't particularly like him."

"If I remember correctly it was all about the same things we were finding out," Cheri said. "He sort of got other people in trouble but no one could pin anything on him, and I wonder if Mr.

Ellis finally did? Maybe something from the past, do you think? Maybe he finally had proof of something Duke did?"

It was a motive. "If my mom had known anything, I expect Daisy would have found out," I said. "It's not like she's shy about her opinions."

"So not many people knew, which means we have to figure it out. I'll find out if Mrs. Ellis is in Atlanta with her kids or if she came back or who came back to claim the body. Then if no one's around, we'll break into their house and search through papers to see what we can find."

"We can't just break into a house," I said.

"Oh they do it all the time on television. It's easy. I think you can get a set of lock-picks pretty easily or I can just use a hairpin and we'll be in. I'll call you later," Cheri said.

I sighed, rolling my eyes. There was a good chance Cheri would find out something else and forget this particular idea. At least I hoped so. I had no desire to break in anywhere. It was one thing to consider getting into Marty's after she died because I could get permission from Daisy, but it was another to consider breaking into Mr. Ellis's.

I started searching online for history at the high school. There were some alumni boards and I started reading through stories on those, hoping that something would give me an idea.

I realized I didn't know what class Duke was in. I had to look that up. It took a bit of doing because of how he locked down his social media. Smart, if you ask me, but also annoying. At any rate, I did see names I recognized, so I could figure it out. Living in a small town isn't all bad.

I also figured I'd search for Mr. Ellis's name. It would be interesting to see what other students thought. Maybe he'd gotten less creepy as he'd gotten older.

That was easier, as the school had reported Ellis's death and people were talking about their memories of him. The announcement about Duke had some nice sympathies, but no memories of what he'd done. I paused to wonder what it might mean when no one shares memories of you. I couldn't image not sharing my favorite memories of Gram or Marty when they'd died.

I was pondering that when Cheri called me back. I was surprised that she'd found out something so quickly.

"My mom knows the woman who lives next door to the Ellis's. The house is just a few blocks from ours if you remember. I always hated it when Mr. Ellis would drive by while we were walking home if we were just standing around talking and we were supposed to be home. He'd always honk?"

"I remember," I said. As always, just slightly creepy but not really out of line.

"Anyway, they took the body to Atlanta and he's going to be buried there. I guess his wife is just going to live with the kids until she gets a place in a senior living center or something. His son will be out to start packing up in a month or so. My mom volunteered along with several other friends, but for now the place is empty."

"Did you also get a key?" I asked. "Because I don't have lock picks and I don't know where to purchase a set, and you can't pick a lock with a hairpin."

Cheri chuckled. "I have a key. Mom's friend is watching the place and she said I could go in and water the plants for her. She has arthritis and she knows we're not like going to go stealing anything or vandalizing things."

I sighed. It sounded like I was going to get to go visit Mr. Ellis's house.

Chapter 20

I drove to Cheri's, watching my rearview mirror for the police car that seemed to know where I was at all times. I hadn't mentioned this to her. I'd have to do something about it before we took off for the Ellis's. I mean, bad enough we were sort of breaking in. We didn't need the police there with us.

There aren't too many apartments in Seales. Cheri lived in one of the few little complexes within the city. There were two rows of six townhouses, and at the end of the big square parking lot sat a low building of one-bedroom flats. When I was a kid, this square had been a sort of cul-de-sac of eight or ten duplexes built in the fifties. They'd gotten so run down that an investor had come in and rebuilt the whole complex. That had happened while I was gone, but Cheri had kept me appraised of the situation as she saved her money to move into town.

The townhouses were three bedroom and quite nice, but they were spendy for the area. The flats were a great deal with all the niceties of the larger units, but with a price that was affordable to someone on a barista's salary.

The townhouses were red brick with white siding, white trim, and black doors and shutters. The flats were the same, but those windows had no shutters on them. About half of them had Halloween decorations in the main front window, and one of the town homes appeared to have gone all out with a sort of entry tunnel in dark black and signs that said 'do not enter.' The parking lot was still in good condition and the dumpster was over in the space between one of the townhouses and the flats, just far enough that no one should be subject to any smells that might leak out from there.

Cheri had recommended I look into this place when I couldn't live in the carriage house. When Marty had challenged the will, I'd been kicked out of there. Instead, I'd lived with my folks, thinking I'd wait until I knew what was going to happen. I could easily have done worse, and even with a will challenge, I'd have had enough funds to afford one of the townhouses.

I parked and looked around. The police car was driving on past, very slowly, probably watching to make sure I got to a door. I hurried to Cheri's and knocked. She was ready to come out, but I pushed her back inside.

"Cops," I whispered.

"What?" she asked.

"You know since I almost got hit, Byron has been having an officer keep an eye on me, to keep me safe. Basically I get followed no matter where I drive," I said. "You'll need to drive us over to your mom's and then to the Ellis's."

"I already have the key," Cheri said. "I just got back."

Which meant she'd probably texted me when she was halfway to the apartment. While Cheri texts when she needs to, at least she generally pulls over and does it so she doesn't cause an accident. The roads around here are all country roads, not very wide, and with speed limits that no one obeys.

I nodded. Her apartment was warm and cozy, and I hated to have to go out again. She had a large living area with a wall of kitchen cabinets to one side of the door. Beyond that was a bedroom with a decent sized walk-in closet and a bathroom that was roomier than you'd expect in an apartment of that size. A stacked washer and dryer were in a closet just outside the bathroom.

The floors were a gray vinyl plank that I wouldn't have picked for myself, but they went with the paint on the walls and the dark gray cabinets that could easily be refinished when they started to look dated. The granite counters were a low-grade granite but likely to wear through just about anything.

I smelled coffee and eggs. Cheri doesn't do much more cooking than that. She loves making her own coffee, which seems strange since she does it all the time at work. Apparently working at a coffee shop had made her very particular about how she took her coffee, even if it wasn't fancy coffee.

After a few minutes where we took turns playing spy and peeking out the blinds that covered the big window in the main room, we slipped out the door. Cheri's car is a gray Ford Focus. It's pretty comfortable. It handles well for most things around here so long as you weren't in much of a hurry.

After turning on the heat, which Cheri warned me would take a few minutes to warm us up, we got started. We drove through Cheri's neighborhood, which is mostly made up of small homes, some with basements, that were built in the fifties. There were a few more duplexes down a couple of cul-de-sacs, too.

We wove our way up the low hill upon which the town of Seales was built on. We avoided the one traffic light in downtown and drove through another neighborhood of post-war houses that looked the worse for wear and tear, finally emerging into a slightly newer neighborhood of ranches and split-entry homes on hills. We passed the street my folks lived on and kept going. Cheri lived about a quarter of a mile away in a neighborhood that was newer still, though new meant only about forty years old rather than fifty or sixty.

Her parents lived in a two-story house that they'd had since Cheri was in middle school. Before that they'd lived in our neighborhood in a split-entry house. My dad often joked that they loved stairs far more than we did. My father was the one always tagged to go running down to the basement for things, and we teased him about his hatred for stairs.

As we drove by, I noted that Cheri's family's big old oak tree had lost a huge branch in one of the last windstorms. Cheri had mentioned it, but I hadn't been by to see it. While Cheri often went to see her mom, I was in the neighborhood less often. My folks came to Gram's house, which, since it was now mine, meant they came to me.

Cheri's parents' next-door neighbor had one of those inflatable spiders on a large front porch.

Its long black legs were weaving in the wind, hanging just over the rain gutters. It made me smile. Other homes had pumpkins and a few appeared to have lights, though they weren't yet on. It was possible some people had left up Christmas lights all year long.

Cheri made a left turn and we went up two blocks until we got to a little cul-de-sac. The houses here were smaller though they were of the same era as Cheri's folks' home. They were all ranches, but not quite so sprawling. The Ellises had a nice little place with a long, white-columned front porch. The façade of the house was in old brown and black brick that had faded to beige or gray in some places. The bushes were overgrown and starting to look a bit disheveled with branches sticking up and out.

The yard was tree free, though most of the other houses had one in the front yard, all old and so large that in the summer the Ellis house probably got just as much shade as any of the others. Cheri parked up the street and we hurried down the sidewalk, which was cracked and in once place slightly raised up, probably thanks to tree roots.

"If you've got a key, it's not technically breaking and entering," I hissed.

"I know," Cheri said, "but if someone is watching, I don't want them to notice us."

If they were watching, likely they had already

noticed us, but I wasn't going to point that out. So close to getting there, I was eager to see if we found something, hopefully a signed note from the killer threatening Mr. Ellis, though I doubted that would happen.

I looked behind us, listening to a dog bark, slow and steady barks suggesting it just liked the sound of its voice rather than the urgent "There are people breaking into the neighbors! Beware!"

Cheri fiddled with the lock while I looked to see if anyone was looking out windows, perhaps wondering what we were doing, but other than the dog, there seemed to be no one around.

Cheri finally got the lock to turn and we stepped into the house. It was cold in there, almost colder than the outside, which surprised me. Of course, the heat wasn't on very high and the house was closed up. It would feel chill, having caught the chill from the nights. The days weren't warm enough to warm it much, either.

In the dim light, I saw a wall off to the left and then a large room to the right with an old wood stove huddling in the corner surrounded by a brown brick surround. The floors were beige carpet, rather new, though the entry was in wood laminate, light colored but in the dim light I couldn't tell what color.

"Do you think it's okay to turn on the lights?"

Cheri asked. “I do have permission, technically, but I don’t want to draw attention.”

“Let’s turn on a light in the back. That way we can see but it won’t be so obvious in the front.” The blinds were drawn, but they were the old plastic mini-blinds that let in plenty of light from outside even closed. If the sun weren’t setting, the idea of lights wouldn’t have been needed.

I followed Cheri through the living room, past the sofa that was big and thick and overstuffed though the cushions sagged in the middle. It had been well-used but cared for. The television was a flat screen, large but not the largest. I noted the pictures on the wall only by the greens and blues and browns rather than subject matter or kind.

The kitchen needed to be redone, the pine cabinets looking worn, the laminate counters scratched. The black appliances were a stark contrast to the pale laminate. Gold knobs and handles were scratched and dull. Everything looked as if it needed a bit of love but was still working, still holding up.

There were no plates on the counter or in the sink. Mr. Ellis had either cleaned up before leaving or someone had done so after he died. Chances were the former, particularly if he had planned to be out of the house for any amount of time.

The kitchen was in a corner with a peninsula with plenty of cupboards over it facing either a large eating area or a small family room. The Ellises had a table there but nothing else. Beyond was a hallway that went to the bedrooms. Cheri had already started down it, turning on a hall light instead of a kitchen light.

There was no desk in the kitchen as they'd often done in that era. I knew this having looked at plenty of small houses in Washington when I thought about purchasing a house instead of renting. I knew I'd be going back to Kentucky, but I liked the thought of being a homeowner and such an investment would have drawn me back there.

I hadn't ever gotten around to purchasing and I can't say I regretted it. I had so much on my plate here at home that I don't know how I would have gone about fitting in a cross-country trip as well. Not that I would have had to. Barb would have been happy to look after the place for me so long as I sent her a Beers of the World subscription or something. But still, I'd have had to pay a management company to find tenants and do the real managing, so it would have gotten complicated.

I noted that the kitchen and area off it was done in pale laminate wood. The light from the hall showed a few scratches, but overall well kept. The Ellises clearly didn't have a dog. The hallway had carpet again, the same beige as up front.

From the lack of wear, I was guessing it had been put in fairly recently.

I followed Cheri down the hall. The first door on the right went to a bedroom complete with a full-sized bed, probably for guests. The door on the left was a bathroom still done in blue and cream ruffles and matching wallpaper.

A large set of doors opened onto a closet laundry, and the next room was another bedroom, smaller than the first holding a desk and file cabinet. This was the room we wanted. If there was something, it would probably be here.

"Maybe I should do this room and you can search the master," Cheri said.

I knew what she meant. If there was something in the office, it might be something that logically made sense. If I touched things in the master, I might pick up something about the owner.

"I'll start there and come back and help you here." I walked to the last door, on the left side. A queen-sized bed with a heavy pine headboard with bookshelves was the centerpiece of the room. The shelves were filled with photos and a few clear cut-glass animals that would easily fit in the center of your palm. A dresser with a mirror was across the room to my right. On it sat a few old Precious Moments figures, probably collected new.

The bedspread was purple and green. The

walls had no wallpaper here, just the off-white paint. On either side of the bed were two nightstands, each with two full drawers and one narrow drawer. Neither side gave any indication of who slept where.

A door to my left led to an en suite and a closet. I ignored it but was thankful that I could turn on a light and likely no one would notice. Even if the bathroom hadn't been there, I probably could have. The blinds here were heavier blackout shades.

The overhead light wasn't as bright as I might have liked but let me see things a little more clearly. The bedspread was more worn that I had noticed at first. I walked to the nightstand closest to me. I opened it, seeing a nail clipper, a few bookmarks with religious sayings on them and a woman's watch.

Probably the wife's side.

I moved around the bed, letting my hand trail on the bedspread. I felt sadness, a sort of resignation. There were no images, nothing strong, just a sort of day-to-day sameness that wouldn't ever change.

I shut down my talent for the moment. The vagueness was almost more depressing than the actual feeling.

I opened the nightstand on the far side of the bed. More nail clippers, an awkward thing that from the tiny hairs inside appeared to trim nose or ear hair. No bookmarks, but an old news magazine was placed inside. I opened it, expecting to find old articles but only the cover remained. Inside were typewritten pages.

My hands shook as I started to read them, thinking I had found something.

Instead, it appeared to be a story. A young man in school uses a magic talent to get away with crimes, hurting people. The narrative was engrossing, and I could imagine it being published if Ellis had wanted to. Instead, it was just there in the drawer.

I flipped through the pages, thinking I wouldn't have time to read it. It was at least thirty pages long, perhaps more. I let my fingers feel the papers, running them over the words, wondering if I could pick something up. It had been printed on a printer, a modern printer, so this was a recent story.

I knew that.

I felt the sense that the story was true, but that it wasn't exactly true. The magical parts were input, the children changed. The people hurt were not the real people hurt. The real boy had gotten away, though in the story I knew he'd come to justice. I felt a real sadness and anger in the writing. There were no exact images. Ellis hadn't been emotional when handling the pages. I got the impression that the emotion was in the story. And it was a story, one that was finished in those pages.

I bit my lip. I wanted to read it, but I also needed to search the room. If the story held any clues, I couldn't just take it with me, either.

I put it back and looked through the drawers.

The first held socks. The one on the bottom held t-shirts. I ruffled through the socks, thinking that there was no underwear there, which seemed odd, but I didn't organize the room. Nothing beneath the socks. Under the t-shirts was a printed bank statement for a savings account that held over a hundred thousand dollars.

"I think I found something," I called to Cheri.

No answer.

I hurried out to see her facing an older man who held a bat, ready to use it. His face was lined, his eyes sad. He was breathing heavily as if he'd overexerted himself.

"Who are you?" I asked.

"I think the better question is who are you," he said. His voice was low and gravely, and he paused between each word as if speaking were difficult.

"I'm Ash Jericho. My friend Cheri and I were asked to look in on the house," I said, hoping Cheri would fill in with her mom's friend's name.

She didn't, but that didn't matter.

"Don't care. You picked the wrong time to do

it. Now get back there." He gestured with the bat that held a swing that suggested that he might be breathless and old, but he knew how to use the thing.

Cheri and I backed up towards the master bedroom.

Chapter 21

I walked as slowly as I could, letting Cheri go ahead. Cheri was clearly terrified, so I wanted to put as much distance between her and the baseball bat-wielding man as I could.

I smelled something sour from him as he herded us towards the bedroom, bat balanced and ready to swing. The bat was an old silver one with black tape around the grip that seemed to be coming off.

Cheri hurried inside the master, practically running towards the bathroom. I followed, hoping we could barricade ourselves in the bathroom only to find there was only a pocket door between the bedroom and bath. The pocket door didn't even have much of a lock, just a flimsy plastic thing to give the bathroom user the sense of privacy. It certainly wouldn't stand up to someone as determined as this man appeared to be.

"What were you two girls searching for?" the man demanded, coming into the bathroom with us, pushing the pocket door aside like it was nothing.

Cheri was pushed against the sink on one side and I was against the closet across the way. The closet was a walk in with folding doors, so no help there, either.

Wind rattled the house. Just what we needed, a small storm blowing up when the car was parked down the street.

"We were told to look after the place, so we came in to make sure nothing had been touched," Cheri said. "How did you get in?"

I wondered that myself. It wasn't as if I'd heard anyone come in.

"I've got a key and I know how to use it," the man said. "I didn't hear about no girls coming by."

"Wasn't planned," Cheri said. "Last minute. I like to be thorough and I brought a friend with me in case I ran into someone like you."

"And what were you searching for in that office?" the man asked.

"Not exactly your business," Cheri said.

"Kind of makes your story out to be a lie," the man said.

"Who are you?" I asked. "Because when we call the police about a man in the house, I want to have a name."

That gave him pause. He clearly didn't expect that we'd be willing to call the police when we'd been found in a house not our own.

"Ain't required. You're the ones trespassing. You go and find that phone out there and call them."

I pulled out my cell phone and started to dial, but the bat slammed my fingers.

"What the hell?" the man asked.

"I was going to call the police on my cell-phone," I said.

He looked more confused than he should have for a moment and then his eyes cleared and he narrowed them.

"No one's calling the cops. You don't belong here. If you had any idea about what you were getting into Ash Jericho, you'd have left well enough alone, but you're a nosy one, aren't you?"

"Not sure what you mean," I said. It worried me that he knew who I was. Why was that? "Maybe if you explained or said who you were?"

"I'm Bud Quint," he snapped. "I was coming by to check up on some stuff. Ellis and I were in business together."

I raised an eyebrow. If Ellis's sudden increase in income had been surprising, it seemed even more surprising that Bud Quint was also involved. I found it hard to believe their business was anywhere near legal.

Bud glared. He was holding the bat tightly, his fingers were turning white, something I noted even in the dim light. He hadn't turned on lights while he was in the house. He couldn't have come in after us, we'd have heard him. Which meant he had to be there before us.

"You were already here," I said. "Where?"

Mentally I thought back to the layout of the house. There was a door towards the back of the kitchen. In a house of this era it might have been a basement. Some of the homes around here had them, even if they weren't walk outs.

Bud said nothing, but he started to tap the bat against his hand and mumble to himself. It suggested he didn't intend to murder us, but it also didn't mean he wouldn't if he had to. He was thinking.

"Why was Duke murdered?" I asked.

Bud looked at me then, eyes sort of watering. He shook his head at me as if he didn't want to answer. The grip on the bat seemed to loosen for an instant as if the very thought of his son made him weak.

"That's why we're here," I pressed, my gut

telling me that that was the way to go. "Was he supposed to hurt Kelly Ellis and something went wrong? The wrong person found out?"

"Leave it," Bud said. "You're too late to help him. You're only going to get yourself killed."

"Someone already put Deena in the hospital. She worked at the pizza place. She might have seen something, but if she did, the police don't know it. I've been followed. Someone was hiding on my property and I think they were trying to put me in the hospital, too." I hoped that maybe giving Bud faces to the danger would get him talking.

"They already know you're asking questions. Get out. Leave town for a month or until this quiets down. They'll move on, too."

"Who is they?" I kept pressing. Cheri put a hand on my arm as if she sensed something about Bud. I didn't look at it, but mentally made a note that maybe I was missing something.

Bud sniffed a little and then bent over at the waist, the bat hanging loose.

Cheri scurried out, getting past him so she was no longer trapped. I followed but I turned.

"Who is it, Bud? Who murdered your son?"

"I can't…" Bud trailed off. "Bastards from Lexington, and I need to go there regular like. In town. And…"

Then he started crying. I started forward to

touch him, but Cheri pulled me back. She put a finger to her lips.

She pushed me out of the bedroom, stepping quietly while Bud doubled over and sobbed his heart out. I wasn't quite sure what I'd said to make him sob like that, but they were deep sobs, the sort that won't stop once they've started, the sort that I'd heard from Daisy after Marty had died.

"What did you find?" Cheri hissed at me in the hallway

I told her about the paper as she drew me back to the kitchen.

"He was in the basement, you thought?" Cheri asked.

The door down was ajar. We both looked at it. We looked at each other. Bud moved around in the bedroom.

I thought about being trapped down there.

"Not now," I said.

We hurried out the door. The wind had picked up and I thought it was probably going to rain later.

Cheri locked up the house, sighing.

"I have to return the key and there's no way I'll get to use it again."

"Is the hardware store still open?" I asked. Off the main highway was a little mom and pop hardware store. Chances were they made keys. We could get a copy.

Cheri grinned. She pulled out a phone and looked at it. "We need to hurry."

Chapter 22

Otto's Hardware sits on one of the old country roads just off the highway. From the highway you pretty much just see the parking lot, which is an oblong shape where the road comes in at a sort of y-angle rather than directly perpendicular. The blacktop has no markings any longer and people park pretty much as they want. The building is low and flat and smaller than most of the big box hardware stores.

Otto's doesn't sell lumber. For that you had to go to the lumber yard next door. At that time of the evening, the lumber yard was closed. It had shorter hours because about the only people who went there were builders. They opened at seven and closed at four. I had a patient who worked there, and he always came in for one of my early evening slots.

The traffic on the highway wasn't heavy as we pulled into a nearly empty lot. A big, shiny black Dodge truck was in the parking lot. That and a smaller, battered white truck were the only other cars in the front. The workers parked in back, which was where a loading dock sat. I didn't envy the large trucks that made deliveries back there. Getting in and out was tight enough in a car. I couldn't image a semi, though I knew they did it.

The scent of fresh wood reached my nose. It was already mostly dark, only the faintest tinge of pink on the horizon still, broken up by gray clouds that were slowly heading towards us. Now and then I heard thunder off in the distance, which seemed to be getting closer more quickly than the clouds suggested.

The windows on the hardware were partly covered by paper advertising. In other places they were covered by palettes of items stacked up higher than the windows. The light inside was so faint, if it weren't for the small lighted "Open" sign, I'd have worried they were closed.

Cheri and I walked in. Otto's didn't have an automatic key-making machine like some of the chain stores did. We'd have to ring for a person to help us at the little station halfway up the main aisle. Cheri did so, looking like she was in a hurry.

A woman with heavy dark hair and darker skin reached us. She sized us up and said, "What?"

"I need to have this key copied," Cheri said holding it out.

The woman took it. Said nothing and got to work. It took only a minute.

She led us up front where she took Cheri's money and that was it.

She said nothing else.

"At least it wasn't expensive," Cheri whispered to me.

"We're cheap here," the woman called, clearly listening to us.

I glanced back.

She smiled at me and nodded. "Yeah, I speak English."

I tried to think what we had done that made her think we thought anything different, but I couldn't.

"You two looked so worried, like you didn't think we'd communicate," the woman explained.

I almost wanted to laugh. Such a simple explanation. "Actually we were worried you'd be closed or not have someone to run the machine."

"Like a man," the woman said, apparently determined to make us bigots of some sort or another.

"Like anyone," Cheri snapped. "Come on. We

need to return this. Maybe Bud will have left by now too."

"If you mean Bud Quint, you watch yourself. Talk about a man you don't need around," the woman said.

"You know the Quints?" I asked, moving back.

"Sure. He comes in here regular. Does some woodworking now, mostly hobby stuff, but it's real fine work. Won't find better in the area. He's done hope chests and chairs and things for people across the country. They pay big money for it. He probably keeps us in business."

The woman had crossed her arms at chest level as if she were proud to know something we didn't.

"Sad about Duke," I said.

"He's an asshole. Apparently Bud isn't as good with kids as he is with wood."

I chuckled a little at her expression of the problem.

"He work with Kelly Ellis in his woodworking?" I asked.

"Ellis painted and stained. His wife did some stencils and distressing. They were saving to move to Atlanta."

"Did they do anything to make someone angry?"

The woman narrowed her eyes. "Think there

was something to that? That Bud might be in danger?" She clearly cared about Quint.

"He seems to know what's going on," I said. "But he won't talk."

"He wouldn't," she said. "He's not one to ask for help. And I think he feels guilty about Duke. He and Ellis had a falling out, but he wouldn't say why. They just stopped coming in together. Ellis stopped coming in here at all, so if he needed any more paint or stain, he was getting it elsewhere."

"Thanks," I said.

The woman nodded, still watching us, something both suspicious and hopeful in her gaze.

"Tell Bud to talk to me if he won't talk to you. I got friends," the woman called after us.

I wasn't at all sure if that last was a kindness or a threat. If it was a threat, I wasn't sure if she meant to threaten me or Bud.

I hurried out, just in case she was going to share with me exactly what she did mean.

Chapter 23

Once in the car, Cheri put the new key on her own key ring. We sat inside waiting for the heater to warm the car up. It made a fair bit of noise in the background, a heavy blowing sound that made a low growl every fifteen seconds or so. At least the heater *worked*. We hadn't been inside long enough for the windshield to fog, but we needed the time to recoup and decide what was next.

"What do you think she meant?" Cheri asked.

"I don't know. But the woodworking sounds like a way to make some extra money."

"You said Mr. Ellis had a hundred grand in a savings account. Do you think he made that much?"

"Hard to say. I don't know what handmade

wood furniture goes for. I also don't know how good Bud was. Besides, why would he be at Mr. Ellis's house if he did woodworking and the two were just sort of in business together? And even then, why not tell us? Who were the guys from Lexington who probably murdered Duke?" I asked.

Cheri sighed. She put both hands on the steering wheel, though the car wasn't in gear, and leaned back, pressing her body into the seat. Then she let up and spoke. "Maybe Ellis was adding drugs to the furniture. Then they'd ship it and people would only think about the furniture?"

"You think Mr. Ellis is our own Walter White teacher breaking bad?" I asked.

Cheri laughed at the picture. Mr. Ellis was about as conservative as they came and the idea that he'd go off and suddenly start cooking meth just to buy a home seemed ridiculous. It was easier to believe he was a rapist or a pedophile, but even then his creepiness was more of the Stephen King sort than the actual criminal sort.

"Maybe growing pot," Cheri said, "but I can't imagine that it brings in that kind of money, not unless his basement covers half the neighborhood. Even then, it's legal in so many states as to not really be worthwhile."

I had to agree with her. It didn't make sense.

"Could they be smuggling something else?"

"Like what?" I asked.

Cheri sighed. "I guess I'm thinking about people smuggling things out of a country. State secrets. Too many movies. Where would Bud and Mr. Ellis get state secrets? We live in Kentucky."

Neither man was involved with the government, either. Duke might have had something from his job, despite Cheri's boss's denial. I didn't believe it, though. Maybe they did just sell furniture. Maybe they were moving drugs even if they weren't making it. It didn't quite feel right, but it didn't feel wrong either.

"What else do you do with wood and paint?" I asked.

Cheri shrugged. "I should return the key and then we can see if Bud has left."

"Let's go," I said.

The streets were starting to get quieter—not that streets around Seales were ever busy—but as darkness fell what traffic there was got even less as people made their way home to dinner or to out to one of the restaurants. Even on Saturday night unless there was a parade or something going on downtown, you didn't get much traffic around town. Get closer to Lexington and people started having social lives where they went out and about. Seales, however, was still primarily a farming town with a side order of government workers from Frankfort.

Cheri drove carefully but quickly through the backstreets of the town until we got to a sprawling ranch a few houses down from her folks. This would be the keeper of the keys, I thought, mentally smiling at the name.

"I'll be right back. I just need to drop these," Cheri said. She hurried out, leaving her keys in the car and the heater on without waiting for me to say anything.

I guess I was waiting. I pulled out my phone and played with it while she talked to an older woman on the front porch. They didn't chat long, though I could see that Cheri was being invited inside. She demurred, pointing at the car. I quickly looked back down at my email though there wasn't anything there.

I didn't have a single message from Thad. I decided to text him instead and see if he'd answer that way. I'd done so twice before. Still, three might be the charm. I was closing my text messaging screen and moving on to sending him another email when Cheri got back in the car.

"She talks so much!" Cheri said. "She heard that Mr. Ellis's son is coming back next week to clear out the house. She didn't expect him so soon, but he wants to get things over with before December comes around, and they want to sell the house quickly so that his mom can move to Atlanta. They were pretty set on moving anyway, the

Ellises, I mean, but now Mrs. Ellis can't bear the idea of coming back. I guess Mrs. Ellis was just on the phone and the two had a chat, so I just got lucky and had to hear all about it. Thank God you were in the car or we'd be in there with hot chocolate and cookies or something like that."

"Well, now we maybe know why Bud was there tonight. Maybe everyone knows that the Ellis family wants to get out of there quickly so they're coming by." I bit my lip wondering if this was such a good idea. Surely Byron had gone through the house already and he'd have noted the bank statement, right? Or maybe not. It was in the bedroom, not the study, which was sort of weird. And it was hidden, at least a little bit. Why was that?

"Why do you suppose he had a bank statement in his nightstand drawer instead of by the paperwork on the desk?" I asked. "I mean, I assume you did find other paperwork?"

"All sorts," Cheri said. "He got everything on paper still." She carefully signaled to pull out onto the street even though there wasn't another car around. "I saw all his regular bank stuff which showed deposits from a pension and social security and then some irregular deposits of a few hundred here and there, but not often. He had some small stocks and his wife had a personal IRA probably from when she worked."

"So nothing like the statement I saw?" I said.

Cheri shook her head. "But you said it was in the bedroom? I mean, that would be odd."

"Sort of hidden, too," I said. "Like he didn't want anyone to know about it."

"Maybe he was hiding it from his wife? Maybe he wasn't supposed to have it?"

I thought about the suggestion. I didn't get any tingling sense of it being the truth though, the back of my neck feeling nothing. I'd been too excited to find it that I hadn't even thought about using my powers to see if there was something attached to the paperwork. I should have. I should have opened myself. Of course, Bud had been there so he might have interrupted me before I learned anything useful anyway.

There were no cars in front of the Ellis house. The lights were off inside. Cheri and I looked at each other before getting out of the car, again. If we did end up getting hurt, Byron was going to be more than a little pissed off at me when he found out what I'd been doing. First, this was a police investigation even if they did think Mr. Ellis's death was an accident. Second, we'd already been caught once in a situation where we could have been hurt.

My stomach started to tie itself up in knots. I really didn't want to get more involved in the investigation. It was too easy to mess up things with

Byron. I mean, I knew that I probably wasn't messing things up as in us breaking up, but I liked where we were now. I didn't want that to go backwards.

It was darker now, not just because the sun was fully set, but because the clouds were covering the area. I could smell the rain coming. I huddled in my jacket while I walked down the street with Cheri.

"Do you think people are talking about us?" she whispered.

"Doubtful," I said. "No one ever watches the street anymore. I mean, most houses don't even have televisions in the front rooms anymore."

"Some of these do," Cheri said. "The Ellises had a front room television and they could have watched outside."

"Then the neighbors will probably see Bud as well. I don't see any other cars that look like they don't belong. I wonder where he parked. It's not like he's in great shape to be walking around."

"Maybe he snuck through a backyard?"

Closer to the Ellises', I noticed that they didn't have a fence. The yard next to them just had a low split rail fence with wire around it. I didn't see what was behind either of them, but if it was a similar setup back there, even with Bud's health problems he could probably get over something that low.

I shrugged. Cheri unlocked the door again. I hoped no one was watching, otherwise they'd probably be calling the police seeing this was the second time we'd been there. If so, we didn't even have a legal key to say we had permission.

I couldn't see anything in the house this time. We had to turn on the lights even though people would see we were there, if they happened to look out and notice. I doubted they would. Still it felt risky.

I walked into the kitchen and opened the far door. I had thought it was a pantry, but it was actually a set of stairs going down. I turned on that light and started down. Cheri was right behind me.

There was another switch at the bottom. We were in a big room that opened up off to my left. It had an ugly brown carpet and a bar and a sofa. The television down there was the projector kind that had a screen hanging down on the wall. I saw speakers in the corners. Mr. Ellis must have loved his TV.

"So much for something illegal," Cheri said.

To my right were doors. Not unexpectedly, the first went to a powder room. I tried the next and it went to a larger, unfinished room. I was about to back out thinking that it was just storage, but I couldn't quite make out what was in there. Tall racks held odds and ends like a typical long term homeowner might have.

Still, I fumbled for a switch, which I finally found on the second open beam to my right. When the lights came on, I wandered around, finding a small space between the racks and the wall. Beyond, I wasn't quite sure what I was looking at. There were printers there and fancy inks and stuff.

"What the heck?" Cheri asked. "Why have a second office down here? And hidden?"

"It looks like it's artwork?" I said. I had ideas, but that couldn't be true. I walked further into the room which stank heavily of inks and dyes. Under the table was a box. I opened it and there was a pile of what looked like ten-dollar bills. Hardly any creases at all, like new.

I dug through it. Who got a pile of ten-dollar bills? Bills that most people didn't look at a second time because tens weren't typically counterfeited. They'd pass through most scans at stores.

Suddenly the pieces fell into place. Ellis was using the furniture he worked on with Bud Quint to send out counterfeit bills. They probably sold the furniture to get it out there, placing some cash here and there. If there were people dealing, say on one of the person-to-person marketplaces selling them, they could pass a lot of bills quickly as they "made change" for real money.

It could bring in a fair amount over a couple of years if they were careful.

I pulled out my phone to take pictures.

I couldn't very well talk about all this stuff, but I could show the photos to Byron. It wasn't exactly like we were breaking and entering. We'd been given a key. And I wouldn't tell him about the copy of the key.

"Can you believe this?" Cheri said, looking around now. "Is it really counterfeiting? I would never have guessed it of Mr. Ellis. It's almost like having your own Walter White except he made money instead of meth."

The door at the top of the stairs slammed. Cheri and I looked at each other.

I hurried upstairs, but while I could turn the knob, I couldn't force it open.

I stepped back a step on the wooden stairs that creaked in ways I didn't like and noticed smoke coming through the underside of the door.

We were trapped and there was something burning upstairs.

Chapter 24

I stood shocked a moment, certain the grayish fog that was gathering at the base of the door must be something else, but the smell of burnt candle and the slight heat I was feeling told me otherwise. Whatever was in the house was burning fast and hot.

I raced down the steps, barely taking care to be sure my feet didn't miss any of the steps. My hand gripped the rail on the wall hard in case my speed sent me flying head over heels into Cheri who was standing at the bottom.

"They've lit a fire," I said.

"Oh my gosh. Oh my gosh." Cheri began to breathe too quickly and then placed her hands on her stomach, something I'd seen her do before.

That seemed to calm her and she had a moment to think.

"There's a bathroom over there. Towels. We can wrap our faces in them and help keep out the smoke."

I remembered the room. It was just a small powder room. If there was a shower, maybe we could hide in there, and as things burned around us, we'd have a certain level of safety. Opening the door, I saw it was only a toilet and sink.

I thought about placing a wet towel under the door. Unfortunately, the smoke was coming from the floor above us as well as under the door. Soon enough that would burn through, sending burning boards down into the basement.

I looked around the room. The windows were all thin casement windows. They slid open. I thought we might be able to get through them, though they were narrow.

"I think we can maybe get through the window over there," I said, pointing at the nearest one. We'd just need a way to boost ourselves up.

The sofa was big and chunky and didn't look easy to move. It was one of the old-style over-stuffed ones. Brown wooden handles suggested the ends reclined.

Those sofas were always heavier. It'd be hard to move on the carpet. We'd have to stand on the back to get enough height for the window. There was a chair in the other room, but it was too low.

"The sofa is probably our best bet," I said. "We can place it against the wall and stand on the back."

Cheri was already moving towards it. It was a sectional and we didn't know exactly where the thing split, so we both started pushing against it. The short half came off. Cheri's end. I moved over there, and we pushed and pulled it towards the window.

Upstairs the floor creaked and groaned. I heard the crackle of flames.

I smelled smoke strongly now. We had to hurry.

I hoped that the outside of the house wasn't also on fire.

It seemed to take forever with every single heave moving perhaps half an inch across the carpet.

"There was a rug by the base of the stairs," Cheri said. "I'm going to get that so we can hopefully push this onto it, at least part of it, and pull the rug across the carpet. My dad did that on that big entertainment system we used to have before he got the flat screen television."

I pictured the big oak system with the doors. It was beautiful, but it was also solid wood. If the rug idea worked for that, we could probably push the sofa around that way.

Cheri returned with a small entry rug and I lifted the one end of the sofa about an inch. It wasn't as heavy as I had expected. Maybe we could have carried the thing over, but we were already working this out with the rug.

Then Cheri grabbed the end of the small rug and started to pull while I got on the other end of the half sofa and pushed. It started to move faster.

Behind me, some wood dropped. It wasn't a large piece, but smoke began to work its way into the basement faster.

The lights went out.

I had my phone and I pulled it out to give us some light. It made pushing the sofa awkward, but we were close enough to the wall to make it work.

"My purse," Cheri said. She ran across the room to the other part of the sofa where she'd dropped her things and grabbed it. I had mine strapped across my shoulder. I climbed up on the back of the sofa, disliking the way it wobbled under my weight. It wasn't secure without its other half.

Nonetheless, I climbed and started working on opening the window. My fingers felt for the lock.

I started working at it, trying to open it.

At first nothing moved. I tried again, pressing the lock out. It was sticky but I thought I had it. I tried to move the window, but it didn't move. Years of neglect, probably.

I swore.

"Hurry," Cheri said, unnecessarily.

I was doing my best.

My hands were starting to shake and my heart was pounding way too hard.

I thought I heard the sounds of things breaking upstairs.

"Maybe we need to break the glass," Cheri said.

I didn't want to chance the fact that we'd rip ourselves to shreds on any leftover glass in the frame. The space was going to be tight as it was.

I kept working on opening the window.

Finally it opened an inch. I felt it give suddenly and then stop.

It wasn't sticky so much as worn. The window that needed to slip seemed like it was stuck in dry dust rather than stuck to another part. I gave it a bang with my hand on the other side as I pulled.

That gave another inch.

Meanwhile the basement was starting to get smokier, especially close to the ceiling where I was. Letting in air was probably not the best thing to do, but we had to get out or we'd die down there.

Cheri was starting to cough in earnest. I didn't know if she was more susceptible or if I was just closer to fresh air. I couldn't quite see us squeezing through that little pane, so I gave it another shove and finally it was as open as it was going to get.

I pushed the screen out onto the ground. At least that was easy.

Then I had to try and get through the opening.

It required boosting myself up and pushing through the opening, leaving me lying on my face in the dirt near the house. At least I wasn't battling bushes.

I thought I heard people over the noise of the fire.

I probably should have yelled for help as I crawled out, but I was breathing hard, wiggling my way through the opening.

I got mostly out and then my butt got stuck.

I am not particularly heavy, but even those of us without much extra weight flare out around the behind. I tried to pull myself, but I was stuck.

"Push!" I yelled at Cheri, hoping she'd hear.

I flailed about for a bit longer and then felt her hands on my butt. At first nothing happened. I felt something rip on my pants along the back of my thigh. I was too much in a hurry to get out to worry about it.

Then I was moving again, and I landed on the ground.

Cheri was trying to boost herself up and

through but was having trouble. She was coughing harder and harder.

When she got her head through a little, I turned and grabbed at her arms, pulling her halfway out.

Then someone tackled me from behind, pulling me away.

I turned to fight, but it was Thad.

"What the hell?" I demanded as he backed off, moving around me towards Cheri.

Chapter 25

I turned to grab Thad, but he was already pulling Cheri's arms towards him, getting her out of the basement. Around me there were sounds of sirens wailing. Blue and red lights flashed. There were people around, some half-dressed, but others were in work clothes. I felt the chill through my torn jeans.

Smoke filled my nose. I coughed harder than I had in the basement. In the open air, the smoke was moving around wildly and everything smelled like a bonfire. It was so strong I tasted the smoke in the back of my throat, which made me cough and choke even harder.

I was doubled over before Thad got Cheri out of the basement window. We were on the side of the house, near the neighbors. The grass there was trampled and worn. A few small bushes lined the house next door but only gravel reached this close to the Ellis house, perhaps to keep foliage away from the basement window, practically the only window. There might have been one in the unfinished part, but Cheri and I hadn't explored that side enough. Even if there was a window, it could easily have been covered up so no one looking in would see what they were doing down there.

"Are you okay?" Thad asked.

I looked at him. He was dressed all in black, from his jeans to a hoodie. Thad isn't the kind of guy who dresses all in black. Even at Marty's funeral he had on a colorful shirt to make a statement.

"I'll live," I croaked out between coughing.

Cheri was coughing as well.

I started towards the front, but Thad pushed us towards the backyard. Actually, he herded us towards the neighbor's backyard where it was quiet and less smoky.

"What's up?" I asked. "What are you doing here?" I wished I sounded better than I did, barely croaking out a sound, breathless and fragmented.

Thad looked around like he didn't want to be seen.

"Are you part of this?" I hissed. Hissing seemed to make sense given the shape my throat was in. It also came out easier. I needed water to cool my dry and scratchy throat off, but I needed answers, too.

Cheri was covering her mouth and nose with a wet towel that she'd gotten. She had brought one for me, but it was left behind in the basement. She wasn't coughing quite so much and when she did, it wasn't loud and hacking like mine. If Thad were trying to hide us, I was sure to give us away.

Thad shook his head, moving us further into the shadows of the backyard. All the yards here were large for the size of houses. The neighborhood had been built in a time when people wanted a yard for their kids and didn't think twice about mowing.

There were a few trees beyond the house and bushes lining the back. The people who lived there liked their gardens. I noted a raised bed, now empty of everything but a final trellis of peas.

"Lucas let something slip the other night, after your detective talked to him," Thad said quietly. "It wasn't like I could go rushing to the police with it, but it was something, you know? Something I thought about but wasn't sure how to tell you. Then things got weird."

"Weird how?" I asked.

Thad sighed. "Lucas hadn't been in town long, maybe six months? He showed up just after Sean and I had broken up for the second time. I wasn't going to go back to Sean or anything, but it's Sean, you know? And Lucas knew Sean, so I made sure I got to know him. Really, I thought maybe they were together or something, but then Lucas took an interest in *me*."

Thad emphasized the last word like it surprised him.

"I don't normally go for the bad boy or anything, but Lucas wasn't all bad, you know? More that soft insides kind of guy. I was so wrong about that."

"What exactly made you think he might be involved?" I asked.

"He said something about a white truck left beside the road. I didn't think the police would tell him that, you know? I didn't ask more about it because you'd been there with Duke and all. And then he said something about those brakes should have gone out too and they didn't."

"He was talking about Duke's brakes? And he was mad they didn't go out?" I asked, hoping to get clarification from Thad's ramblings.

"He didn't say it like that," Thad said. "Sean was there, and he looked really mad about it. Hurt maybe. But it made me start wondering what they were into. I didn't want to go to the police if there wasn't anything there. This was *Sean*."

"Why didn't you answer my calls?" I hissed again. I was mad now because I'd been really worried about him, wondering what was going on with him and where he was. I'd worried that someone had gotten to him for talking to me.

"I didn't have anything to say," Thad said. "Besides, Sean was around a lot more. He and Lucas were always holing up together. I was feeling really insecure thinking the guy I was going out with was going to leave me for my ex, which was just like the worst thing I could think of. I didn't want to dump that all on you when I didn't know anything. You know I would have."

Thad would have. He falls deeply in love at the drop of a hat and nothing can persuade him that the person might not be good for him until he gets his heart broken. There's something to be said for loving the way he does. I can't imagine going through the pain he goes through every time someone dumps him. I've not even been that close to him, but all those wounds leak over onto his Facebook page and into even casual conversation, though I know, mostly, that he's trying to put a good face on it. Emotionally, he just tends to be dramatic.

"Today, this Craig guy came by and was all pissed off at his girlfriend over something. I guess she was supposed to hit someone with a car and didn't do it and he was yelling at Lucas. I was in the bedroom. I guess he didn't realize that Lucas wasn't alone. They just stopped, not just talking but moving, when they saw me. I thought they were going to shit a brick. I just smiled and said something about the fact that I was certainly glad she was okay and I could understand the upset, like I totally misread them. I left for work after that and I haven't been home."

"How did you find us?" I asked.

"I read about that teach Mr. Ellis dying as well as Duke. They said something about the teacher's kid in one of their discussions, so I headed out here, thinking about Mr. Ellis."

"And?" I asked. "Why are we here instead of in the front with the emergency responders who could probably get us some water and check to see if we need to be hospitalized?"

"Because Lucas is out there and he doesn't look happy," Thad said. "He's pacing around the front and talking on the phone. He lives in Lexington. Why is he even here?"

"Maybe you should tell me because you're the one who brought us to someone else's backyard." I was fed up with Thad's attitude. He knew something and he wasn't saying. He acted as if this was all some cloak and dagger movie instead of a situation where people were getting killed.

"I don't know," Thad said, stomping his foot like he was a toddler instead of a grown man who knew better.

I stared at him. I looked for my bag, but it wasn't there. I had the straps from it, but the bag itself must have been ripped off when I'd gotten stuck in the window. Cheri had left hers in the basement as well. So much for a phone.

I swore, quietly and under my breath. I had hoped to call Byron, knowing that he was someone I could trust.

"If you can't tell me why I shouldn't go out there, I'm leaving now," I said to Thad.

Cheri stood up straighter preparing to follow me.

"Please," Thad said, grabbing at me.

I hated to do it, but I slipped by him without even looking back. If he wouldn't tell me what he knew, and I was fairly certain that even if he didn't know something he had a good guess, I was going out front. It seemed a whole lot safer to be surrounded by police and firemen than it was to be in a dark yard with a man who might or might not have my best interest at heart.

As I tromped through the grass, I realized I would never have guessed that I felt that way about Thad. Normally he's as true blue as they come.

Was there something going on with Sean? Was Lucas threatening him?

Just as I had that thought, a woman appeared at the side of the house. She was dressed in a dark blue sweat jacket, no hood, and dark jeans but blue not black. She wore a black pullover under the jacket and her hair was brown and tied back.

"I'd stay there," she said. She had no weapon I could see, but there was something in her stance that made me pause. She might have been tiny, but I sensed she knew how to fight.

"Why?" I asked. From here, I could scream. Surely someone would hear me. Surely one of the neighbors would glance over. We were halfway to the front of the house.

"Because I said so," she said. "Thad won't like it if you go out there and let them all know you survived. Right now there's just a car that's been called in as yours so they know you're probably here. But you won't be leaving."

"Actually, I was doing just that," I hissed. I worried I wouldn't be able to scream loud enough.

That thought was taken away when the woman rushed towards me, jumping at me, pushing me back. If I had any breath in my lungs it was lost when she landed on me. I tried to draw a breath, but she clamped a hand over my mouth and drew a knife.

Fortunately, Cheri didn't see the knife and she was already screaming, not as loud as I would have liked, but I hoped it was loud enough.

Chapter 26

The knife didn't move from my throat, although the woman moved around so that she was facing the front of the houses. I didn't dare sit up any further, so my vision was of dark swirls of black against the night. There was just enough light to make out that there was plenty of smoke. I felt heat coming from the Ellis house, but it seemed be centered in the back of the house, probably near the stairs. I'd seen firefighters in the front, working as if there were flames there, too. Had they tried to keep Cheri and me from going out that way as well, just in case?

Fortunately, no one had thought to block my escape window, or maybe they had and that's why it was so hard to open, though I suspected disuse was probably the reason. At least it had worked, finally.

Cheri was still screaming as much as she could, but it sounded forlorn and sad against the sounds of rushing water from the hoses and the chatter of people and radios and the running of engines. Like a kitten trying to get attention in a wildfire, I thought.

Yet I heard the noises changing, felt as if there were people walking closer.

"What's going on here?" someone said. A man.

Cheri kept screaming.

The woman had a hand over my mouth.

"Her name is Stephanie. She and her friend Craig and his friend Lucas are holding my friend Sean hostage and now they're threatening to kill Ash," Thad said. His voice was surprisingly steady.

"He's an idiot," Stephanie snapped. "I caught her trying to spill fuel on that fire and I'm holding her for the police."

"She did not." That was Cheri. Not as hoarse as I was, but not exactly her usual self. "We were trapped in that basement, where I had a key and it was known I was in there, when someone locked the basement door and started a fire on the first floor. We had to crawl out that window."

I imagined Cheri pointing, but she was out of

my range of vision where I was stuck with a woman with a knife that smelled like blood. What else had she used the knife for?

Stephanie didn't argue. "Stay back." She ordered whoever was there. I wondered who was talking to her. A neighbor or the police? If it was just a neighbor, would they get the police?

Something crashed in the house. Fortunately, the side yard was far wider than most modern ones, but the crash let out a burst of heat. I felt sweat on my forehead. It could have come from the knife at my throat as easily as the heat.

"We need to get out of here," the voice said. "You could all die."

"Better that than having to go back to jail," Stephanie said. It wasn't yelled. Just quiet and firm. Great. She wasn't going to just let go.

"It's over, Stephanie, don't you get it?" That was Thad. He was agitated.

"No, I don't get it. We can all burn up here for all I care," she snapped.

"Just stop. I told you I'd find them. I didn't think you were going to kill them, just distract them like you did before," Thad said. "The whole thing with Duke was your idea, wasn't it?"

"Shut up," Stephanie told him. Her knife wavered a bit. She hadn't yet cut my throat, but I worried that she'd make a mistake and I'd end up dead anyway. Had it been like that with Duke?

Then I remembered all the things wrong with his truck. Someone wanted to be sure he died.

"No," Thad said. "Ash is my friend, too, and I'll keep talking so long as you hold that knife to her throat. I know I wasn't supposed to know all of this, but I do, and you can't just kill me now that the police are here watching you try and murder someone else. They know."

"Shut up. Shut up. Shut up!" Stephanie said, getting louder on each set of words.

Thad said nothing.

Then I felt Stephanie being pulled off me from behind. I moved her arm so that the knife passed above me.

I had a vision of a young girl who needed something, though I didn't know what. I had a sense it wasn't Stephanie, maybe a daughter? She was pretty and innocent and sweet, and there was some level of shame attached to the little girl. A frustration. A sorrow. Then the arm was out of my hand, pulled away by the tackle.

I heard an ommph and sat up and looked around. Cheri was on top of the Stephanie. The knife had fallen to the side.

Police were moving around me. I got a glimpse of Byron hurrying to Cheri's side, leaving me there. In another instant, he was beside me, having made sure others were taking care of Cheri and Stephanie.

"I do not even want to know what you were doing here tonight," he muttered. "Can you stand up?"

I nodded and let him help me. That brought on some more coughing. He led me over to the fire engines and someone found me water, a nice cool bottle of water which I drank as quickly as anyone would let me.

There were plenty of questions which I tried to answer. Cheri was better at it. The wet cloth had allowed her to keep more of her voice. She was croaking out responses better than I could.

Thad was quiet and he kept looking at his feet. I understood that he'd been trying to help Sean, but at the same time I was angry that he'd put me in danger. We'd talk about that soon enough.

Byron, however, wasn't letting Thad off the hook. He kept asking about Sean. Thad had no idea where he was. Lucas had disappeared and Stephanie was definitely not talking.

When an officer led her towards an ambulance, I saw Stephanie glare at me. I shuddered. She was not a happy camper.

"We've sent someone from Lexington to see if her boyfriend Craig is around," Byron said. "I don't know if he will be or if he'll have gotten word. Lucas is missing, so he could have called him. They could both be in the wind."

"What about Thad?" I asked. I did not ask about Sean. Let Thad do that.

"We'll be questioning him more closely, but as near as I can tell, he doesn't know that much. He's been poking around, worried about his friend Sean, who may or may not be involved in this. I don't have a clear picture around that."

The medics wanted to load me and Cheri up to go. We were both ready, although I wasn't keen on heading to the hospital. Still, it couldn't be helped.

Chapter 27

Fortunately for me, hospitals don't make you stay too long anymore. There's always the worry that the insurance companies are going to complain that they're over treating and over-billing. Leaving sooner was not going to be soon enough for me.

The place echoed with mumbling voices. The bright lights and shiny white tile floors were hard on the eyes. I was given something to soothe my throat immediately as well things to take home. Everything came with an order to see my regular doctor the next day.

Apparently, I passed all their tests. Cheri's mom came and got her moments before I was released. Walking out, I was met by my folks in the waiting area. Neither of them looked happy.

"I never liked that Thad boy," my mother said as we walked through the dark parking lot to their car. The emergency room was at an awkward angle on the hill, so we had to walk down the hill towards the parking area. The lot was brightly lit. I heard the sounds of traffic, despite the hour, on the street beyond. Some roads are always busy.

"It wasn't Thad's fault," I said. "His friends knew I knew some people here, and they were trying to get information."

"He locked you in that house," my mother insisted.

"No. He pulled us out of that house. The woman, Stephanie, locked us in and tried to burn us out or maybe it was that guy, Lucas."

"But he was there because of Thad."

"I'm not sure that's true," I said. "I think they had been there earlier, probably following Bud Quint to see what he'd do."

My mom shook her head. She was determined to blame Thad. I had a feeling nothing I said was going to change that. My dad patted me on the shoulder as we all got into my mom's car. My dad was driving, of course. My mom wasn't going to drive to Lexington, which was where the hospital they'd taken me to was located, in the middle of the night.

I got in back and tried to pretend to be half

asleep and not listen to her chatter on with half-truths and gossip.

"And Cheri!" That got my attention.

"Can you imagine her getting that key from her mother's friend and sneaking you in there? I would not have expected that of her, but it just goes to show that you can always tell when someone comes from a lower class."

"It's Cheri," I said, an edge to my voice.

My mom opened her mouth, but my father cleared his throat. That was enough to make her rethink her whole spiel. Not that she could do anything about my friends. I'm an adult and I don't live in her house, so it wasn't like she could forbid me to see them.

She crossed her arms. We rode the rest of the way home in irritated silence. I kind of watched out the back window, but the headlights behind us changed and moved and there didn't seem to be a particular car that followed us. Most cars passed us quickly on New Circle Road and then on 60 out towards Versailles. The traffic got lighter and lighter. By the time we turned off onto the highway to take us towards Seales, we were nearly alone on the road.

That was when I really started paying attention. No headlights came rushing up behind us to run us off the road though. My dad drove carefully, his hands always at two and ten, his head facing towards the front at all times. Even when he'd cleared his throat, he'd held the car on the road like he was on a mission.

I was nearly asleep when we turned on the road to Gram's. At some point I was going to need to start thinking of that as my house. It was strange to be riding with my folks to her house when I lived there. My car was at Cheri's and Cheri's car was probably still over by the Ellises', unless her mom dropped her so she could pick it up on her way home. I was going to need to beg a ride over to Cheri's in the morning to pick up my car.

I was not going to ask my parents for a ride. My dad would have done it and not said much, but my mother was busy trying to place blame on someone for what had happened. I was tired of listening to her.

We were turning into the driveway at the house, paused while my dad pressed the button to open the gates. I started when headlights came towards us.

They rode high on the ground, like a truck or an SUV. I held my breath, wondering if they were going to turn into the driveway and hit us. My shoulders tensed. I knew on some level that was the worst. If we got hit from behind, I'd be in better shape if I were relaxed rather than tensed against the impact.

But after that night, I couldn't help it.

The car was coming fast. The gate was opening too slowly.

My dad seemed unaware of the issue, and he wasn't in any hurry to get onto the property beyond the gate.

He slowly set the car moving forward. The headlights were practically on top of us. They were coming so fast, I wasn't sure how they'd make the turn onto the driveway.

Then they were past us without turning. The white SUV just kept right on going.

I let out a breath, trying to keep it quiet. But even then my mother looked back at me like she knew there was something I was keeping from her. I said nothing as we continued up the driveway to the house.

While there were lights near the gate, the main part of the drive was dark. I saw the front porch light on. I wondered how much Morgan and Daisy knew. It probably depended upon how much my mother had said if she'd called Daisy.

As the drive curved to go around the side of the house, I saw that all the house lights were on. We had a bright one for the side door. Given what had happened when Jaci was working out of the barn and I thought I'd been chased, we'd made sure it was bright. There was another at the back so that the whole area was lit up.

Morgan must definitely know what was going on. I hoped that he hadn't waited up for us, but as I got out of the car, he was there holding the door.

"Are you staying?" he asked my folks.

"We're not far," my dad said. "No need to trouble yourself."

My mom said nothing. She was definitely not pleased, which was something I'd have to deal with in the morning.

"You didn't have to wait up," I said.

"I was worried. Your dad called here to let me know you were at the hospital. Miz Daisy was calling around to find out what was going on, and we both heard a lot of things. I'm glad you're okay."

"Thanks, Morgan," I said, heading into the house. Win wasn't up, but she'd left a note that there was soup in the fridge and ice cream in the freezer. I wasn't hungry, actually, and went to get some water. I'd warm it and let it slide down my throat. To be honest, the ice cream sounded good, but I had a feeling that I'd regret it later. The coolness might help my throat, but I wasn't sure about the sweetness.

I climbed up the stairs. I planned to tumble into bed before deciding that even if I couldn't smell it, I probably stunk of smoke. I didn't want to wake to that. I tossed my clothes in the hamper and took a long, hot shower.

Chapter 28

The next day, Byron came over and we sat in the office talking. I found that the front office with the greens and creams and pale wood was the best place to chat if I didn't need everyone in the house to overhear. Of course, they would listen to a certain extent, but it made it harder. I could probably close the door, but I'd already sat down and didn't care to get up.

Win had outdone herself in soups. I had four different types of chicken soup, which she deemed as the most soothing. Some had more chicken and heavier spices, and others were lighter, more brothy things that could be drunk down in a mug. She kept after me to drink as if just by drinking enough of that stuff I'd cure any problems my throat might be giving me. I have to admit it was relaxing.

As a result, the whole house smelled of chicken soups and spices, and my stomach growled for something heavier. I wasn't sure I wanted anything heavier going down my throat no matter what my stomach said. My throat was still scratchy and sore like I was trying to get a cold. I wondered if the things I'd do for a regular sore throat would help ease it, but I hadn't felt motivated to try. Almost getting murdered in a house fire takes a lot out of you.

Which meant that by the time Byron got to the house, I hadn't done much of anything. I was in my sweats resting, with my eyes closed on the sofa in the great room. I had called patients to reschedule appointments for the next few days and that was it. Daisy was out and about, and I hadn't quite paid attention to what she was doing when Byron arrived.

It took more effort than it should have for me to get up and chat with him in the study.

"News?" I asked. I could talk. I wasn't quite so hoarse, but I was protecting my throat as much as I could.

Byron nodded. "We got a lot of information from Thad. It doesn't appear that he was involved. We also verified that Lucas was threatening Sean. We found Sean, by the way. He was over with Bud Quint. The two of them had been tied up in Quint's house. They weren't hurt. Quint seems to think that Lucas needed them alive in case they were needed for leverage. I'm not sure who they thought they might leverage with Bud, though. He isn't quite sure either.

"It's possible Bud was expected to watch Sean, though after what they did to Duke, I'm not sure why they'd trust him," Byron said.

"Maybe they had something else on him. Lucas was from out of town wasn't he?" I asked.

Byron nodded.

"Ask about Bud's daughter. Maybe Lucas knows something about her that could harm her in some way."

"I'd thought of that, but we haven't gotten anywhere with that line of questioning. Bud just clams up."

"Too bad. We could probably help him."

"Stephanie isn't talking, at the advice of her attorney. We're thinking that perhaps Lucas and Craig are trying to get out of the state. Her silence may be helping them. From what we've gathered from Bud and Thad, Craig and Lucas were the movers and shakers."

"Lucas came to town and started all this, didn't he?" I pressed. I remembered some of what Thad had said about Lucas coming in and being such an amazing guy and changing everything.

Byron shrugged. "Lucas knew Craig slightly. Craig's always been a petty thief. Lucas was into bigger stuff. In fact, he found Ellis and started the whole counterfeiting operation. Craig knew Duke Quint and talked him into getting his dad to make furniture. Apparently Bud has always done some woodworking. Bud didn't know about the counterfeiting at first and was getting taken for a ride on the money. Duke figured out what was going on and told his dad. Bud got mad and started demanding a share."

I nodded. "Is that why they killed Duke?"

Byron shook his head. "Ellis was getting ready to move and wanted out. He had the money he needed to get a home in Atlanta near his kids. Duke was supposed to run him off the road and make sure he was injured too badly to move any time soon. I think they had some hope that the injuries would push Ellis into using that money for expenses as well."

"But why murder Duke?"

"He didn't like the idea of hurting someone. He knew his dad had health problems and worried that as soon as he wasn't able to build furniture that he'd be eliminated as well. Besides, Duke wasn't that involved. I'm not even sure he approved of what was going on. He could have been pressuring his dad to just quit. Hard to say. What we've got comes mostly from Bud. Tough to verify.

I got the impression from what Stephanie's not saying is that they decided to take Duke out while he caused an accident to make Kelly Ellis stay here."

"But Kelly Ellis was killed."

"No one expected the semi would overturn the way it did and Ellis wouldn't be able to stop. They thought he'd just be injured. Duke wasn't necessarily supposed to die, though they made sure he'd be plenty injured. Bud seems to think that they wanted to use Duke's injuries as a warning and scare him into keeping working.

"It doesn't sound like a very a good plan," I said, stretching a bit as I listened. There were still some holes, and I had a feeling that Duke's sister might be one of them.

"I think that to really answer those questions, you ought to find Duke's sister. Do you even have a name?"

Byron nodded but didn't share it. "We're looking for her because we think she's probably a key. I expect she probably knew some people even beyond Lucas."

"Is she in New York?"

"I've heard a lot of different places, so all we can do is keep an eye out for her and for Lucas and Craig as well."

Which didn't sit well with me at all. I wanted this wrapped up. I didn't want to feel like I had last night, constantly looking over my shoulder, wondering who was behind me and if they were going to grab me or try and run me off the road. In all the other situations I'd been in, at least I'd been able to have closure. This didn't feel like that.

I took a deep breath and asked Byron if he wanted some soup.

Chapter 29

Our Halloween party went well, though I was jumpy and worried about someone coming into the house who shouldn't. However, we had a big police presence and all went well. Thanksgiving came and went, and Byron started back to work on the carriage house. I was now able to drive without freaking out if a pair of headlights made the same turn I did.

It was nearly Christmas before we had any news. Daisy and I had decorated the trees. As always, we had a huge twelve-foot tree in the main room. Gram used to have a smaller one in the formal living room, too, which Daisy and I had also done. The big tree had our ornaments and the smaller one in the living room, which had lower ceilings, had a more formal organized look.

This was largely because Gram always hosted a holiday evening social at the house.

Daisy and I decided to hold one this year. We hadn't last year with everything going on. We'd liked having people in over Halloween. The kids in their costumes had been very cute. We'd managed to find someone to do a last-minute maze, not the fancy ones with plants, but one made out of wood with plenty of places for kids to run around in. It had been enough of a hit that we'd probably do it again. Chances were, Seales would require us to do it again.

Christmas would be different. It's a more festive holiday. We wanted people in to see how the house felt with so many folks, mostly adults. Halloween had really turned out the families.

"I know it's a holiday and what not," Daisy said, "and I know that I like people more when it's festive, so I don't know if this is the best way of figuring out what we need to do. Still, it sounds like fun. Even though I'm thinking I'm not up for the constant work of a B&B, I think I like planning events. It'd be nice to have a special place to do that."

Given what a hit the Halloween maze had been, I had a feeling having an outdoor area for weddings could be a hit as well. It would take a bit more planning. Daisy seemed to like that. It would mean people in our space only temporarily, too, and if I had a family of my own someday, then I wouldn't have to worry about where to live.

Morgan let Byron in before he even knocked at the door. Morgan had probably been dusting around the windows and spotted his car driving up.

"What is it?" I asked.

"Got a call from the Cincinnati police. Found the body of a woman named Irene Lux, clearly a made-up name. No record of her. They found links to Lucas Ross. We got permission to do a DNA test on her. It's Darci Quint, Duke's missing sister."

"Oh, my," Daisy said. She looked sad at the thought of a dead young woman.

I moved over and gave her a hug, knowing she was thinking of the family, of what it meant to hear a child was dead.

"We let them know. Cinci police managed to find Lucas and his buddy, Craig. They're being brought to Bram County as we speak. I've been in contact with a number of other departments around the Midwest. Seems they had quite a counterfeit racket going on. It wasn't just Ellis and Quint making up the money, but a whole bunch of folks. They had about fifty different distributors who passed it on a regular basis, mostly selling items that could go direct to consumers who were less likely to remember to check their money or remember where they got it."

"Wow," I said. "Was Lucas in charge?"

Byron shook his head. "Police in Chicago think they have some ideas, but everyone is happy, particularly the FBI, that we had as much information as we did."

"The FBI was involved?"

Byron nodded. "Counterfeiting."

"Were they here?" I asked.

Another nod. "We had all the evidence, so you didn't need to speak to them. They were mostly interested in Stephanie."

Naturally. I sighed.

Byron continued. "When we found Lucas, we found records. He was pretty high up. Reynolds and his girlfriend were just the ones who turned him onto Ellis and Quint. Lucas had been running things here when Ellis decided he wanted out when he decided to move to Atlanta."

"And Duke didn't really want him dead." I said, remembering what Byron had told me.

"They worried that Duke would give into conscience and talk. He and Ellis could back each other up. The irony is that if Duke hadn't died, he probably would have taken the hint and not talked. We'd never have looked into Ellis at all."

I gave him a long look.

"Well, you wouldn't have looked into Ellis."

I smiled.

Win brought in a cup of coffee for Byron, which he accepted gratefully. He took a sip and then breathed out, eyes half closed enjoying it.

"Sometimes I think you like Win's cooking more than you like me," I said, teasingly.

Byron took another sip of coffee, ignoring the jibe.

"Wait until you get Christmas dinner," I said. Byron and I had dated a bit last year at that time but not seriously. He'd missed out.

This year would be our first together. Penelope Blue leaped on my lap for that, purring at me. I shivered a bit because ghost cats are cold.

I thought I heard the words "It could be a very special holiday" whispered in my ear. It sounded like Gram. I didn't usually see human ghosts. Gram told me it was harder to interact with them. I had tried to see her a couple of times, though I'd only succeeded once. I wondered if this was her way of showing herself again.

Whatever. I smiled, a little thankful that we'd had some closure on the final mysteries of what had happened to Duke Quint and Kelly Ellis. Hopefully now I could concentrate on my business and my relationship with Byron.

Author's Note

Anyone who drives through Central Kentucky from Versailles to Frankfort will know I played fast and loose with geography in that area. There is no Seales and no Bram County. However, the town itself was inspired by Woodford County Kentucky and its environs, which residents will recognize.

All of the people are purely fictional. I have taken great liberties with the small police department in Seales and made it fit what I needed.

Ash's friends from Vancouver, Washington, Lisa and Barb, are inspired by friends from acupuncture school and acupuncture practice. Neither of them have had to keep a secret about my psychic abilities because I have none. Like Ash, I miss my friends (not just Lisa and Barb) from the Pacific Northwest, but this part of my life has taken me elsewhere and made me learn that there are many places in the U.S. that are beautiful and have their own flavor.

Enjoy your reading, and if you get a chance to drive through Kentucky, enjoy the ride through some beautiful rolling hills.

About Bonnie Elizabeth

Bonnie Elizabeth could never decide what to do, so she wrote stories about amazing things and sometimes she even finished them.

While rejection stung her so badly in person, she spent most of her young life talking to cats and dogs rather than people, she was unusually resilient when it came to rejections on her writing, racking up a good number of them.

Floating through a variety of jobs, including veterinary receptionist, cemetery administrator, and finally acupuncturist, she continued to write stories.

When the internet came along (yes she's old), she started blogging as her cat, because we all know cats don't notice rejection. Then she started publishing.

Bonnie writes in a variety of genres. Her popular Whisper series is contemporary fantasy and her Teenage Fairy Godmother series is written for teens. She has been published in a number of anthologies and is working on expanding her writing repertoire.

She lives with her husband (who talks less than she does) and her three cats, who always talk back.

Stay in Touch

Also by Bonnie Elizabeth

The Whisper Novels

Whisper Bound

Taken by the Sound

An Air of Suspicion

Little Dog Lost

Death Interrupted

Down in Whisper

A Haunting Whisper

A Haunting Attraction

Secrets Not Whispers

Only Human

Appalachian Souls Series

Souls Lost

Souls Broken

Other Novels

One Bad Wish

Sun Spot Magic

Ghosts from the Past

Unnatural Secrets

Find them all at your favorite bookseller or check us out at MyBigFatOrangeCat.com

www.ingramcontent.com/pod-product-compliance
Lightning Source LLC
Chambersburg PA
CBHW030620310726
48979CB00003B/805

* 9 7 8 1 9 5 3 3 6 3 0 7 7 *